"Business Is Not Sex And Baseball,"

Melanie said.

Sloan's gaze followed a sexy redhead's tight skirt out of the elevator. "Really?"

Melanie took a deep breath and said between her teeth, "Has anyone ever informed you that business should be ethical, clinical, professional and not necessarily finalized or celebrated by sexual marathons?"

Sloan chuckled and stroked her soft, hot cheek. "Try a sexy musk or flower perfume instead of that professional businesswoman stuff. You might catch a date for Friday night."

Her lips firmed. "I'm as capable as you are, Raventhrall. And we both know that someday you're going to pay. Trust me, I won't make it easy."

Dear Reader,

Welcome to the merry month of May, where things here at Silhouette Desire get pretty perky. Needless to say, I think May's lineup of sexy heroes and spunky heroines is just fabulous... beginning with our star hunk, *Man of the Month* Cooper Maitland, in Jennifer Greene's *Quicksand*. This is one man you won't want to let get away!

Next, we have the second in Joan Johnston's HAWK'S WAY series, *The Cowboy and the Princess*. Now, please don't worry if you didn't read Book One, all of the HAWK'S WAY stories stand alone as great romantic reads.

Then the ever-popular Mary Lynn Baxter returns with *Mike's Baby* and Cait London appears with *Maybe No, Maybe Yes*. Maybe *you* won't want to miss *either* of these books! And don't pass up *Devil or Angel* by Audra Adams—just which best describes the hero, well, *I'm* not telling. Next, Carla Cassidy makes her Silhouette Desire debut with *A Fleeting Moment*. You'll never forget this witty, wonderful love story.

Yes, May is merry and filled with mayhem, but more important, it's filled with romance... only from Silhouette Desire. So, enjoy!

All the best,

Lucia Macro
Senior Editor

CAIT LONDON
MAYBE NO, MAYBE YES

SILHOUETTE *Desire*®
Published by Silhouette Books New York
America's Publisher of Contemporary Romance

SILHOUETTE BOOKS
300 East 42nd St., New York, N.Y. 10017

MAYBE NO, MAYBE YES

Copyright © 1993 by Lois Kleinsasser

ISBN: 0-373-05782-2

First Silhouette Books printing May 1993

All the characters in this book have no existence outside the imagination of the author and have no relation whatsoever to anyone bearing the same name or names. They are not even distantly inspired by any individual known or unknown to the author, and all incidents are pure invention.

Printed in the U.S.A.

Books by Cait London

Silhouette Desire

The Loving Season #502
Angel vs. MacLean #593
The Pendragon Virus #611
The Daddy Candidate #641
Midnight Rider #726
The Cowboy #763
Maybe No, Maybe Yes #782

CAIT LONDON

lives in the Missouri Ozarks but grew up in Washington and still loves craggy mountains and the Pacific Coast. She's a history buff and an avid reader who knows her way around computers. She grew up painting landscapes and wildlife—but is now committed to writing and enjoying her three creative daughters. Cait has big plans for her future—learning to fish, taking short trips for research and meeting people. She also writes as Cait Logan and has won the *Romantic Times* Best New Romance Writer award for 1986.

In appreciation of Melissa Senate, a honey of an editor who is destined for a beautiful and long career

One

"**P**eaches." Melanie muttered Itty Bitty's pet name for her as the tough ex-con approached her office.

She snapped the pencil she had been holding when Sloan Raventhrall swung into view. Raventhrall, looking sleek and tall next to Itty's blocky frame, was Melanie's arch rival at Standards Elite, a financial consulting firm.

Itty mumbled around his cigar and Sloan nodded thoughtfully as usual during their Monday morning discussions. The big men moved through the jade-and-mauve interior of Standards like sharks circling baby seals.

Sloan's tailored gray suit emphasized the power of his six-foot-two, athletic body. He projected the business image of a successful financial advisor. Dark brown wavy hair offset a jaw that locked when Sloan gnawed on a problem. Straight thick brows shadowed eyes that liquified female hearts.

A heavy September drizzle had settled over Kansas City, Missouri, suiting Melanie's thoughts about Sloan. His lazy, seductive gaze disguised a man who viewed stocks and bonds as serious fun, and a neat office as his personal destruction zone.

When foraging for a new account, Sloan Raventhrall reminded Melanie of a hunter after prey. He circled the challenges and methodically pinpointed the problems. A genius at tearing aside minor difficulties to get to the real problems, Sloan possessed certain animalistic edges—savage, masculine drives—that set Melanie's teeth on edge. Other women clustered to him.

Her broken pencil fell to the carpet by her navy blue business pumps. Melanie fought the tendency of her upper lip to curl in distaste as she thought about "Sloan's Women." Typically, they were amazons without the slightest idea of how a company merger could affect its shareowners. His last acquisition, a brunette by the name of Lola, thought that the New York Stock Exchange was where cattle were traded.

Client and advisor, the men strolled down the hall with lowered heads. Talking intensely, oblivious to the other Standards Elite employees, Itty and Sloan moved by Melanie's tiny cubicle. Contrasting Sloan's neat, executive style, Itty Bitty's stocky six-foot-three frame was clad in brazen knit plaid. Thick, unruly gray hair and massive eyebrows topped a head that lacked a neck.

Melanie sipped her cup of hot water and fought the headache nudging the back of her brain.

She would trade all of her clients for Itty's challenging account.

Sloan's large hand reached out to lightly slap Melanie's open doorframe, taunting her with his possession of Itty's account and shattering her mental vacation. Sloan's dark fingers rested on the sign marked M. S. Inganforde, the initials an effort to add business beef to her femininity.

She frowned slightly, noting the slight dusting of hair across the back of that big, grasping hand. Sloan Raventhrall was primitive and predatory. Melanie suspected that his business suit could be easily exchanged for a Western bounty hunter's garb.

Melanie gritted her teeth, tugged down the sleeves of her neat navy suit and adjusted the small professional business pin attached to her lapel. Shaking with controlled frustration, she inhaled deeply and straightened the narrow frames of her glasses.

"Hey, Mel," Sloan said easily. Melanie resented that deep, resonant tone that could easily override hers at an intense board conference. Exactly twelve inches spanned the distance from the top of his six-foot-two height to the top of her hair. The carefully constructed spiky hairstyle added a necessary two inches to Melanie's height.

His brown eyes crinkled with amusement, carefully gauging her mood for his next barb. Melanie straightened in her chair, forcing her pumps to stay on the small pedestal beneath her desk.

Sloan shot her that "I'm all male, honey" grin that melted women like wax in a furnace.

She locked her stare on him, primly straightened her papers, and silently recited her affirmation concerning Sloan. *A beefcake sports jockey does not a good financial consultant make.* Or *All good things come to those who wait.* Or basic, old *Good triumphs over evil.*

He blocked her doorway, like a huge Texas longhorn...bull—she decided the matter of sex based on the number of women revolving in his life. Sloan's hard mouth curved slightly as he waited for her to speak to him.

She smiled tightly, hoping that tossing him that polite bone would satisfy his intense need to torment her.

Sloan didn't move, his grin widening as her color rose, infuriating her.

"Go away," she ordered in a husky voice that reminded her of a cat hissing at a dog. She hated losing her carefully practiced business tone and poise, and Sloan darn well knew it. Succeeding again at ruffling her career image, he blew her a kiss before moving off to his office with Itty.

Melanie's fingers shook as she adjusted her business association pin on her lapel again.

She concentrated on the soft rain sliding down the smoked-glass window. With luck she could soothe the nerves that Sloan had scratched since his arrival three years ago.

Sloan's walnut door closed quietly, reminding Melanie of sharks convening for a blood hunt beneath a beautiful coral reef. Or gunfighters entering a smoky saloon.

"Peaches. Honey. Baby doll," Melanie muttered, repeating Itty's names for her, then tried desperately to return to Mrs. Lacey's safe stocks. Melanie blew a long cat hair from the portfolio Mrs. Lacey had been studying at home. The small, elegant grandmother preferred to swim in shallow, secure financial waters and was typical of the accounts delegated to Melanie. Her neat files consisted of minor accounts requiring little tending and creativity.

Melanie ached for blockbuster accounts. Big action in a fast market with a difficult, aggressive client would prove her ability as a top consultant.

Sighing wistfully, she checked her messages to see if her mother had called. Since January, her mother had been acting just a bit odd, giving off faint signals that she might someday become "involved" or married again. The widow of two husbands, Delilah had sailed through raising her children alone and seemed happy enough until lately. Melanie frowned. When her mother arrived, they could sort out the problems during an all-night pajama session.

Forty-five minutes later, the intercom on her desk buzzed, and Sloan's raspy, deep voice asked, "Mel? Can you come in here a moment? We need your expertise on the Mogul Enterprises securities."

Melanie mentally foraged for a way to delay and prepare for the confrontation. "I'm sorry. I'm tied up right now—"

"This will only take a few moments of your time," Sloan said easily. "Itty wants to move on purchasing these stocks this morning."

Itty's barroom voice commanded, "Move it, Peaches."

Melanie took a deep breath and quietly snapped another pencil, dropping it to the light jade carpet. After a long moment, she said coolly, "Very well."

Determined to retain her shredded dignity, Melanie added, "I'll be free in fifteen minutes."

"Make that ten, will you, Mel?" Sloan's voice rasped. In the background, the television sports announcer praised a St. Louis Cardinals outfielder, and Itty cheered.

"Fine," she returned after breaking two more pencils in quick order. She stuck out her tongue at the office intercom, adjusted her pin yet again and lifted her head, focusing her eyes on a painting hanging on her office wall. Monet's delicate brush strokes portrayed water and lilies and slowly soothed her nerves.

Taking a deep breath, Melanie smoothed her hair under in back, then plucked a spiky curl higher on top of her head. She stood slowly, drawing up to her full height, and quickly surveyed her curves at a downward glance.

The navy jacket and skirt with a basic white blouse and collar fitted her with an expensive nuance that was worth the fabric's high cost. Melanie's successful business image pleased her.... She frowned slightly, tugging her jacket over her full breasts, which were minimized by a specially sewn bra. Unfortunately, she had inherited her mother's lush contours, blond coloring and petite packaging. Melanie smoothed her shoulder pads and lapel and decided to add a half inch width to the next jacket she sewed.

To the untrained eye, Sloan's expensively tailored suits and shirts seemed to be just taken from the cleaner's hanger.

But to Melanie, the seamstress, his suits and shirts looked like he'd slept in them.

Or made love in them in the back seat of a— She forced her thoughts away from Sloan's love life. An image of a rumpled bed, amid wrinkled clothing, mirrors and a variety of sounds taunted her for a moment before sliding away.

Melanie rubbed the slight ache at her temple with two fingers. Smoothing her skirt, she checked her hose and the unscuffed shine of her pumps. She pulled open her file drawer with the same force she'd like to have used to jerk Sloan's tie and extracted a neat folder containing her memos on Mogul Enterprises. Assured that her image was totally Sloan-proofed, she took a deep breath and strode to his office. She'd practiced the brisk walk in front of a mirror; it projected a powerful business image.

Melanie clenched Sloan's office door knob for an instant, bracing herself for the assault on her senses. The room would be just a notch above a smoky poolroom.

She closed her lids, preparing mentally for the messy, paper-cluttered desk and the bold Van Gogh painting. Sloan often referred to the artist as "What happens when a man tends his investment portfolio without Standards Elite's advice." Itty's special ashtray, a ceramic license plate he had made in prison, would be filling with cigar ashes that spilled over onto his open, mussed files. A sports game would be playing on Sloan's office television, and in midsentence both men would stop an intense financial discussion to rivet their attention to the game. At that point they would toss batting averages and bets at each other with machine-gun speed.

Along the way, they would hash out Itty's next financial coup.

Sloan would be sprawled back in his oversize chair, feet resting on his desk. He would aim darts at the bull's-eye placed next to a picture of a client "who did him wrong."

Itty's hand-held calculator, which he punched with un-equaled skill, and Sloan's computer screen filled with graphs would portray a business relationship.

Georgette MacDougal, Standards' executive secretary, passed and handed Melanie a phone message for Sloan. "It's from his ex-client's wife. The vamp with the unbeliev-able bumpers. Give it to Sloan, will you?"

Melanie took a deep breath, knocked twice, then braced her shoulder against the heavy walnut door to open it.

Sloan's dart hit the bull's-eye before he glanced up at her. Both men had taken off their jackets, thrown them in a pa-per-cluttered lounge.

"Put it there, Peaches," Itty ordered around his massive cigar. He nodded to an empty chair already dusted with his ashes.

Melanie hesitated, aware that Sloan's keen stare had noted her distaste. She thrust the telephone message onto his desk. Sloan scanned it, his face hardening before he crumpled the paper and tossed it into a small basketball hoop attached to his trash can.

"We can go up to a half a mil in stock," Itty stated, glancing at Melanie. "Sit down, baby doll. We're talking about Mogul Enterprises, and the genius here seems to think you can help."

She sat carefully, leaning back to portray ease. Mogul would be just the company she would choose for her inves-tors, if...

Sloan placed his hands behind his head and wiggled his sock-clad toes. "How stable is Mogul Enterprises, Mel? Their overseas yield isn't what it used to be since the Ramzackies coup."

"They make up for it stateside, and the new board chair-man is innovative and conservative. Mogul should be a good stock. Their diversities override the problems. The new chairman is cutting waste and the company should show third-quarter profits." She smoothed away a cigar ash clinging to her skirt and hated sharing her expertise with a man who infuriated her.

She smiled as he frowned, debating the investment. The dark frown deepened as Sloan stared at her. "When did the chairmanship change at Mogul? How do you know, Mel?" he rapped out, leaning forward in his chair.

Devereau, Standards' chairman of the board, called that Sloan's bird-dog-pointing-to-quail look.

Melanie took a deep breath. "I read past the sports page," she returned evenly as Itty laughed outright.

If there was one small, good particle in her relationship with Sloan, it was that he trusted her professional input. When he asked a market-related question, it was because he wanted to know the bottom line, not that he was questioning her integrity.

When Melanie tried to think positively about Sloan, she pinpointed that glowing moment in history when he picked her up so she could reach a pencil that had rolled to her closet's back shelf. Sloan hadn't made an issue of the event, had skipped reference to her petite stature and had moved away as though nothing had happened. Frequently he reached the paper supplies that were too high for her.

"Two to one that info wasn't in the paper, Sloan," Itty said. "Peaches is sharp for a broad. 'Course I never do business with a broad, but if I did, I'd consider you, Peaches." His meaty hand clamped around the delicate shape of her knee before moving away.

Sloan noted Melanie's quick expression of distaste before she pushed her soft lips into a small smile. She stealthily eased her knee under the hem of her skirt.

Melanie Sue Inganforde wrapped her Miss Priss attitude around her like a suit of armor. When he'd begun at Standards, Sloan had checked the personnel records of his peers and associates with the help of a sexy secretary. He'd been surprised to discover Melanie's five-year marriage and divorce. She looked untouched, secure in her shapeless suit. Maybe that was why Sloan's hand clenched into a fist when Itty gripped her knee. The gesture was a habit of Itty's, much like the manager of a ball team giving a good-luck pat to the behinds of his passing players. But that small, gently curved knee seemed very intimate and virginal; Sloan's instincts rose to defend Miss Priss's delicate, silky skin.

He enjoyed ruffling her smooth, efficient feathers and seeing her temper ignite. But another man's hand on her knee brought out an emotion in him that Sloan did not want to dissect.... Maybe it was a residual effect from his boyhood, when he was ordered to protect his younger sister.

Melanie wasn't his choice for a weekend in paradise, though she could be counted on to meet business challenges and work through nightmarish schedules. Her compact, shapeless little body agreed with the suits she favored. He remembered lifting her to enable her to reach a high shelf; her waist was hard, conforming to the blocky contour of the rest of her body. Now her hand gripped a file containing Mogul Enterprises information as a slender index finger prowled down a list of figures.

Dressed in an immaculately tailored, loose navy suit, Melanie always wore business clothing with buttoned-up collars. In the three years since he'd arrived at Standards, he'd never seen her without a suit jacket or her glasses.

A player who did his best work on a mental level, Sloan eliminated the necessity of itemizing lists that Melanie favored. Her neat, orderly habits gnawed at him.

Melanie disturbed Sloan on another level and he didn't want to know why. He frowned slightly, noting light touches of mascara behind her glasses. Her eyes were a deep cerulean blue, and when she was angry, they reminded him of crackling blue fire.

Sloan traced the vein beating in her throat. The rapid pulse reminded him of his throbbing headache. He'd had a foul morning with Danielle, his four-year old niece.

Dropped on his apartment doorstep a week ago last Friday
by his harried sister, Danielle was intelligent, overly ener-
getic and a cheerful "morning person." Sloan had agreed to
baby-sit his only sister's child because no one else, including her grandparents, could manage her antics. Danielle's
parents needed a vacation on a quiet island after a long and
hard summer.

That Saturday morning Danielle had made breakfast for
him and demolished the kitchen. After that, Sloan had lost
her in the baseball stadium only to find her in the bull pit
writing her name on balls. The coach had not been amused,
nor the pitcher who'd found gum in his cherished good-luck
glove.

Sloan had called off his Saturday night date and a Sunday golfing appointment with an associate.

Monday afternoon his housekeeper had reluctantly agreed
to baby-sit until he could find someone for Danielle. One
week later Maxine was showing signs of strain.

Sloan tried to forget the headache that pounded at the
back of his skull and the way his throat hurt. He inhaled
Itty's smoke and experienced a wave of nausea that he at-
tributed to Danielle's special Sunday night feast of hot dogs
and peanut butter.

He tapped the dart on his desk while Melanie delivered the
bottom line in her efficient, clipped voice. For a small
woman, Melanie's professional tone projected power and
pride. He'd seen her wrangle choice accounts from another
competitor at the Monday-morning board table. He reluctantly admired Melanie's wish to succeed in the male-dominated company.

Sloan shot the dart at the board, and Melanie jumped.
She threw him an icy look of disgust and continued, "Mogul should be good investment material now. It could
change when they merge with Hanford Dynamos by the
middle of next week. Stock will go sky-high then. I'm certain they'll show a profit next quarter."

"So you figure that we should make our move before Monday market opens?" Itty asked Sloan.

"By Friday at the latest," Sloan agreed, feeling slightly light-headed. He opened a drawer and took out aspirin and an antacid tablet, swallowing them while Itty watched the television and did his best thinking. "I miss Stan 'the Man' Musial and good old Leo," he muttered, referring to Leo Durocher, a past manager of the Cardinals baseball team. "Those were guys."

"If that's all..." Melanie snapped the file shut. She stood in her practical pumps, and Sloan wondered illogically what her bare toes would look like in fire-engine-red nail polish.

It was then that he vowed never again to eat Danielle's specialty of hot dogs and peanut butter. "Thanks, Mel. I owe you," he said, slightly unsettled by his thoughts.

She smiled at him icily. "Of course, you do. You always owe me. I'm going to collect someday."

Itty roared with laughter. "Go, Peaches!"

At Standards' usual Monday afternoon conference, Sloan took the chair by Melanie.

"Sit someplace else, Raventhrall. I've had a bad enough day already," she hissed without turning toward him. "There's a catsup stain on your tie. Not that it's ever properly tied."

Sloan glanced down and noted how well the stain matched his maroon tie's paisley print. "I'll live. There's a cat hair on your skirt," he added, just to chip at Melanie's composure.

Actually he didn't think he would survive until the close of the day. His headache had worsened and the thought of Danielle waiting to play horsey made his throat scratchy.

Melanie straightened her notebook and flipped to one of her carefully tabbed sections when the chairman of Standards swept into the room. Justin Devereau looked and smelled like old, carefully hoarded money. He glanced around at the twelve-member team over his glasses and grimaced for a smile. "The market is bullish," he said, noting the rising market prices and buyers interested in purchases.

Mr. Devereau sat at the head of the table and gifted Sloan with another smile. "That was a stroke of genius last week, Raventhrall. Selling out those commodities before Weight Gone toppled. That's why you're Elite's star player. The rest of you, pay attention to Sloan's flexible, creative techniques. Playing a safe game is good standard procedure, but every once in a while, flex those muscles and get those creative juices going. But remember, we at Standards have worked for our quality image. I still doubt Raventhrall's comments about electronic game ventures. Communications seem much more reputable investments."

Sloan did what he knew would rattle Melanie, edging closer until he caught her easing slightly away from him. Melanie never erupted in undiluted anger, though she steamed wonderfully. Sloan waited for the day when he could truly drive Melanie to sheer, passionate, uncontrolled anger. When Devereau rose and turned his back, describing the stock market indexes and trends by using prepared charts, Sloan whispered, "What's in your notebook section marked 'Raventhrall'?"

Melanie flipped open her notebook to reveal a list of dates and notations of every time she'd helped him. "Info for Itty" was marked with six stars.

"I'm hurt," he whispered. "I thought you did all that in the name of love."

She glared at him while Devereau droned on about current trends and bigger profit margins.

Devereau proposed a new package for investors, settled down with his notebook and asked for comments.

Melanie sat straighter, ran her pencil down her notes and adjusted her glasses. Sloan recognized the signs: M. S. Inganforde, professional investment consultant, wanted to input to the conference table. Typically Devereau would sweep aside her comments and move on down the table for other input—male input.

Sloan glanced at the neat check marks and tracked her line of thought instantly. Melanie's career was her business, he reminded himself. If she hadn't discovered by now that she was a token female at the conference table and that Devereau could not toss aside his basic work ethics—

She spoke effectively, organized her thoughts well, and Devereau nodded. As was his custom when Melanie projected her ideas or input upon a current topic, Devereau's jowls sank defensively into his immaculate collar, his hand-woven Italian tie straining at the weight. He twitched once during her short input and when she finished, he immediately said, "Good concept. Make a list for my secretary, M. S. How about it, Sloan? Should new investors at Standards be given the priority, special-welcome package? What do you think about the toy idea—having a professional toy-maker set up a special Standards Elite toy to tutor first-time investors?"

"Good thought. Investing is a scary process for first-timers."

Devereau nodded. "Draw up a list of specs for my secretary, M.S. If the star player thinks it's a good idea, my secretary can spend some time on it."

The meeting progressed into a cool, efficient discussion of "what the market will bear." Melanie's pencil snapped quietly and she tucked it into a pocket of her leather binder. Sloan noted the pencil pocket bulged.

In the elevator taking them down to their offices, Melanie avoided looking up at Sloan. In the crowded enclosure, Sloan stood four inches from her and braced his hand on the paneling at her head to keep from being pushed against her. Melanie resented the protective gesture, yet realized that Sloan's big body could easily crush her.

She closed her lids and forced away the image of crushed, bodacious amazons in Sloan's rumpled, messy bed. She spoke to the elevator button panel. "One of these days, you're going to pay me back, Raventhrall. It's just a matter of time. The Reamer account should have been mine. Of course, I don't play handball at midnight for my accounts."

"Midnight games pay, Mel. You should try 'em," he returned easily, noting how she edged away from touching his body.

Her eyebrows lifted high in a Miss Priss expression. "At least I get my accounts honestly. I hear you tutored Toti Jeffords's wife at the club's tennis courts before you got that account. It was supposed to have been mine. Jeffords and I had arrived at a tentative arrangement at lunch that day."

"Hey, Mel. Be fair.... Don't forget last year when you fixed sushi for those Japanese women investors. The all-night pajama party didn't hurt."

"That was a small account. You got their husbands' business because of the basis of sexual bias of that old-line company. And my client lunch with Jeffords is something that is acceptable in business. Done every day."

"Jeffords wanted you to play ball, Mel," Sloan stated slowly, watching her eyes carefully. Melanie's color rose to a soft pink and her eyes glanced away from his, proving his hunch correct. When she straightened her collar and swallowed, something slammed into his gut and he wanted to meet Jeffords in a very lonely back alley. Maybe he was having an off day, instinctively playing big brother to Melanie.

The elevator door opened, and Sloan deliberately blocked Melanie's path. He smiled down at her. "Say please."

Her blue eyes crackled with angry fire. "I'd rather—"

"Ah...ah, don't be crude," he drawled, delighted with her response. "Why don't you use all that energy making some guy happy?"

Her eyebrows lifted higher. "Business is not sex and baseball."

Sloan's gaze followed a sexy redhead's tight skirt out of the elevator. "Really?"

Beside him, Melanie took a deep breath and said between her teeth, "You're rabid . . . you need shots, Raventhrall. Has anyone ever informed you that business should be ethical, clinical, professional and not necessarily finalized or celebrated by sexual marathons? There are such things as meaningful relationships."

Behind her glasses, Melanie's icy blue gaze swept down the wrinkles hiding behind Sloan's tie. She sniffed delicately. "There are things like cleaned ties, pressed suits, organized lives, separating business and pleasure, Friday night laundry—"

Sloan chuckled and stroked her soft, hot cheek. "Mel, I have other uses for Friday night." He didn't want to think about his promise to take Danielle to the shopping mall. To add to Inganforde's pique, he said, "Try a sexy musk or flower perfume instead of that professional businesswoman stuff. You might catch a date for Friday nights."

She jerked away from his touch. "I detest your condescending, arrogant attitude."

He laughed outright as she dipped under his arm in one of the quick, deft movements that had at first surprised him. Melanie strode out of the elevator and over her shoulder, shot him back a look of disgust. Sparks seemed to ignite off the peaks of her curly hair, which added inches to her height.

Sloan winked to nudge her rising temper.

Her lips firmed; her eyes blazed behind the glasses. "I'm as capable as you are, Raventhrall. And we both know that someday you're going to pay. Trust me, I won't make it easy."

"Sticks and stones, Mel. I'm terrified," Sloan returned, reaching out to pat down her hair. Inganforde's hiss of anger followed him as he ambled out the door toward his office.

"You will be," Melanie said quietly. Then she smiled, adjusted her lapel pin and walked quickly toward her neat office. Sloan watched Melanie's "I'm-going-places" stride, traced the all-business skirt down to the hem and admired the slender curve of her calves. She had great legs, but so far as he had seen, the rest of her charms resembled a bratwurst sausage.

M. S. Inganforde swept into her office, leaving Sloan's nostrils filled with her businesswoman's scent. He frowned, slightly uncomfortable with his protective feelings for her. Rummaging through emotions he preferred not to spend time on, Sloan decided that in another situation, he might have viewed Inganforde as a friend. Generally he preferred to keep women out of his business, unless they were the obvious Hilda the Hun, or the win-some-lose-some, it's-been-nice types.

Sloan pulled a cellophane-wrapped peppermint candy out of his suit pocket, peeled away a napkin-bit notation about the Cardinals baseball team's best hitter and shivered with a sudden chill.

Flipping through several telephone messages, Sloan noted Maxine's repeated pleas for reinforcements. Showing wear around her sturdy edges, Maxine could normally handle storms—

Sloan frowned, the slight movement of his skin increasing the drumbeat inside his head instantly.

His headache pounded heavily when he thought of Danielle waiting for him. He hoped all the hot dogs and peanut butter had vanished. . . .

Two

At five-thirty, Sloan opened his apartment door and Maxine passed him with frantic excuses. Flushed and wary, his housekeeper escaped. A glob of grape jelly trailed down the back of her stocky leg; torn tissue clung to her navy uniform and fluttered to the floor in her wake. Without sympathy, Sloan muttered, "Deserter."

His sprawling contemporary apartment reeked of burned . . . something, and the ceiling-to-floor drape covering a massive window that overlooked Kansas City hung by a thread.

Danielle's familiar toys mixed with Sloan's various new toy-bribes across the lush carpeting and modular couch.

Sloan had never been a fold-and-put-away personality. He depended on his well-paid housekeeper; she provided his comfortable bachelor lair with a balance of food and order. At thirty-eight, he'd fought off a devoted mother, an ex-wife and several potential brides, protecting his kingdom of comfortable sloth. Resigned to her only son's firm bachelorhood, Mrs. Raventhrall had settled for long, wistful sighs on her visits.

His housekeeper happily folded and cooked, and her arrangement with Sloan suited both of them.

Until the arrival of his niece. Last year, at three years of age, Danielle had stayed one week with Sloan. The arrangement with his only sister had proven so acceptable that Danielle's parents had decided to extend the time to two months this year. A baby-sitter had been arranged in the same apartment complex, thus allowing Sloan a moderate amount of free time. Mrs. Lorring had called Sloan at work at two o'clock on the first Monday and had asked for a reprieve. Maxine had valiantly stepped into the gap.

Now, faced with providing for Danielle's care alone, Sloan realized the full terror of pioneers in a wagon train, surrounded by warring Indians. As a last resort, he would place a blockade at his bedroom door.

On the advice of a woman who managed three children and her assistant's job, Sloan had called the top-notch Baby Sitter at Your Beck and Call Agency. They agreed to supply applicants and placed his name on a waiting list. The first free baby-sitter would interview on Wednesday morning. Mrs. Lorring had reluctantly agreed to baby-sitting Tuesday...with the condition that she could call Sloan and he would arrive within the hour to reclaim Danielle.

After a week and a half of bribery, Danielle reigned the queen of happy disorder.

"Uncle Sloan!" Danielle threw herself at his knees and steadily began climbing him as though he were a tree. A pocket of his expensive jacket tore out, a button popped off his shirt. Danielle reached his shoulder and threw her leg skillfully across his shoulders, preparing for her customary horsey ride. Sloan's dry throat ached as he noted dully that Danielle's grape-jelly prints spotted his jacket.

"Now, listen here, little gal," he began in his deepest cowboy drawl. "This old cowhand needs a sars'parillie and some grub mighty quick."

Danielle squealed in delight and began bucking as she rode his shoulders.

Sloan managed a few valiant horsey steps before putting her down. Danielle's big brown eyes lifted to him; his favorite tie clip had been wired to her barrette and hung awry in her unbrushed tangled curls. An Armani tie served as her belt, circling the top of his best gym sweat suit. Maxine's apron formed a ruffled cape down Danielle's back.

Tears oozed over the grape jelly on her cheeks as Danielle suddenly sobbed, "Uncle Sloan, I don't feel good." She reached her arms up to him, stepped closer and said with a sob, "Hold me."

Placing aside his headache and chill, Sloan stripped off his jacket and tossed it to the floor. He crouched to pick up and cuddle the little girl. Danielle lay unusually submissive and quiet in his arms as he sat. "Mama always takes my temperature," she stated helpfully, snuggling deeper on his lap and rubbing her hand on his jaw. "Sometimes she calls the doctor."

Terror raced through Sloan, and he fought panic with a valiant effort. Danielle's flushed face was hot as she stared up at him.

She placed a small, grape-scented hand against his cheek and sniffed. She rubbed his rough skin and tried to smile. "Guess what, Uncle Sloan? I think you're sick, too."

While Danielle dozed in his arms, Sloan managed to call his friend, Dr. Miles Lobella, pediatrician. Miles, also known as El Lobo at the gym and the bachelors' Friday night poker games, arrived while Danielle slept.

El Lobo, dashing and dressed for a night on the town, grinned at Sloan after examining Danielle. He closed the door to the cleaned and sleeping little girl, and the two men spoke quietly in the living room. El Lobo rolled down his dress shirt sleeves and briskly replaced the French cuff links as he instructed Sloan on the use of a thermometer and on recognizing symptoms for serious changes in Danielle's illness.

Advising Sloan of the proper dosage for cherry-flavored medicine, El Lobo said, "It's a kid thing, old buddy. Comes hot and high, levels off on a low-grade temperature, leaves the kid listless and tamed for the space of...oh, say in Danielle's case, maybe half a day. Adults take almost two weeks to recover to full steam. Nothing to do but wait it out. By the way, from the looks of you, we'd better cancel Friday night's game here, huh? See you when you're back in the world again. Sissy's Ferrari is waiting, engine revved, you know.... I'll call."

Sloan's headache pounded and he dropped to the couch, exhausted. An hour later and all through the night, Danielle alternately slept and awoke with fever.

On Tuesday morning, Sloan called his office to say that he wasn't feeling well and wouldn't be working. After cancelling Mrs. Lorring's services, he called his mother. Mrs. Raventhrall, according to her taped message, would retrieve and answer messages from her various stops along the retired persons' bus route somewhere near Boise, Idaho.

Sloan had been deserted before—when his mother left him on the steps of kindergarten. Of course, then, his superhero lunch box always held a bribe....

Danielle timed her fretful periods perfectly; when he began to doze, she awoke. As he took the cherry-flavored medicine with Danielle, Sloan's head began to float—when it wasn't aching.

Near three o'clock the next morning, El Lobo called from a nightclub. Sloan yelled in a hoarse whisper, demanding help. El Lobo displayed his usual sympathy: he laughed louder, yelled at his partner to save a tango for him and slammed down the phone.

Ellen, the shared secretary at Standards, muffled a giggle when he called in Wednesday morning for a sick day. Then he discovered that Beck and Call wouldn't loan out sitters to sick children, as they had to preserve their dauntless reputation.

M. S. Inganforde called in her brisk business tone to relay a message that Itty wanted his account tended. Sloan closed his eyes, focusing on the cool professional image of M.S. Her pleased smirk stayed behind his hot lids. *You always owe me. I'm going to collect some day.*

Itty called the apartment just as Sloan finished cleaning Danielle's latest bathroom devastation.

At one o'clock, Itty called again, sounding like a water buffalo in heat as he demanded his investor's rights. Moving his lips around a thermometer, Sloan managed to pacify him. He scanned the thermometer; his temperature was one hundred and three. He hoped distantly that he hadn't grabbed Danielle's rectal baby thermometer left by his sister two years ago. At five o'clock, Sloan called Maxine who would not accept several bribes, including a trip to Bermuda, to return to the apartment.

That night, Danielle's temperature waned slightly and she sat watching television while Sloan stared at El Lobo's donation of dinner—a package of frozen beef Stroganoff. The beef-and-noodles concoction caused Sloan's stomach to roll.

By Thursday morning, Danielle began hunting peanut butter and hot-dog makings. Sloan roamed the shambles of his apartment in his boxer shorts and T-shirt, feeling like a mariner in the desert, hunting for an oasis.

Itty called later Thursday morning. "I want action, boy. Friday is buy-or-lose day, remember. Better start Plan B, whatever that is. I asked Peaches what to do about your flu and she said to drink plenty of water and juice. The Cards won last night.... Better come up with something, S.R."

Sloan recognized the S.R. term; Itty's bottom line always included personal initials.

M.S.—the initials stood cool and firm and capable, gilded behind Sloan's hot lids. In a pinch, he could count on M.S., professional woman, to replace any given superhero. He dialed Standards, and the switchboard operator transferred him to Melanie. "Mel, I need help. Can you come to my apartment?" Sloan croaked, just as Danielle began clicking television channels wildly and screaming with delight.

"It's five o'clock now, Sloan. Thursday is my night for grocery shopping and going over Mrs. Lacey's accounts.... My mother is visiting soon and I'm neatening up my apartment. I couldn't possibly come.... I found a note from Susie Dunkirk in my file on communications—the one you borrowed. A little old for kiss-kiss mush, aren't you?"

Sloan grimaced, his head throbbing and light. Through a parched throat he managed, "Please, Mel?"

The long pause that followed finished with the snap of a file folder closing. "I cost big, Raventhrall. What do you want?"

"Itty's file, my phone-number black book and a legal tablet under that potted, dead fern. There's a napkin with figures on it in a blue file in my top drawer and a Cardinals program with notes stuck somewhere... in *C* for Centipede Electronics—" He paused, drank a long sip of sweetened fruit drink from a clown cup and sniffed. "I don't feel well, Mel. My niece is..." he hunted for the word to describe Danielle's tyranny "...better. You think you could baby-sit while I worked on Itty's accounts?"

After a long silence, M.S. said firmly, "I don't do children, Raventhrall. Tough."

"Bring the account background. Itty is in a snit. Standards wouldn't like losing his account," Sloan said, trying a threat.

"Itty's not my account, remember?"

"Bring the damn background material, Mel. I'll give you anything you want."

Sloan imagined Melanie's eyes narrowing behind the large glasses as she schemed. "It will cost," she said after a moment. "And cost big. Do you want ice cream?"

Sloan debated and cherished the thought of cool ice cream sliding down his hot, parched throat. "Well...maybe cherry nut, with real chunks of cherries and real walnuts," he rasped. "It's my favorite."

"Vanilla for a sore throat, Raventhrall," M.S. stated ruthlessly before she hung up.

While Danielle punched telephone buttons to create her favorite nursery songs and managed to converse with children at long-distance rates, Sloan dozed. He savored the brief respite from her role as a nurse.

Finally Danielle slept, looking like an angel in his guest room, and Sloan crawled into his bed to rest.

The phone rang and Sloan reached for it quickly to prevent it from awakening Danielle. Itty's barroom voice cracked across the line. "What's going on, Raventhrall? Friday is action day, you know. Call me."

Melanie pushed open the unlocked door. "Sloan?"

"Sloan?" she asked again, moving cautiously into the dark depths of a gloomy, frightening cave. Clothing lay strewn across furniture. Golf clubs had been arranged around the chrome table to resemble bars on a cage.

Her knee hit a tricycle, and Melanie edged past it, cradling the grocery sacks against her for protection. She stepped on a rubber duck, whose slow squeal of pain caused her to jump. Melanie carefully placed her business pumps on the carpeting. When she lifted her foot, a purple-stained paper stuck to the sole. The kitchen, marked by dirtied expensive pots and pans, loomed around her as Melanie placed the sacks of groceries on a table. She gasped slightly, spotting the jelly, peanut butter, burned eggs with matching shells, mixed with slices of torn bread, crusts firmly removed. She retrieved the bags and inched them to a counter that was somewhat cleaner, though littered with various emptied cans.

Stealthily making her way through what appeared to be a war zone or a blockade, Melanie discovered Sloan sprawled across his bed, dressed only in his loose shorts.

Sleeping fitfully, he cursed Itty with a hoarse, painful sound, then flopped onto his back.

Sloan Raventhrall, scruffy with a beard and tousled hair, amid a fever, would appeal to any woman, Melanie decided sourly. Long, muscular legs, sheathed in tanned skin and light fur widened into narrow hips, covered by flocked cotton shorts. The elastic waistband dipped low to expose his navel. Working upward, her gaze slid across a broad, muscled chest covered by a wedge of black hair.

Melanie swallowed, unable to move as Sloan flopped back onto his stomach and mumbled Itty's name restlessly.

The loose shorts cupped Sloan's tight rear accommodatingly and muscles rippled across his back as he nuzzled a king-size pillow. A teddy bear fell to the floor amid a stack of animal cards. A koala bear with a large bow around his neck that resembled Sloan's best Italian tie, lounged on an unopened briefcase. An expensive pottery lamp lay cracked in pieces, though someone had valiantly attempted to mend it with cellophane tape.

Melanie stepped back from Sloan's dark lair strewn with shirts, slacks and various athletic gear. A golf club braced against the wall slid to the floor, blocking her freedom.

Stepping over it, she turned to see a small girl with masses of curly black hair. Woeful brown eyes stared up at Melanie. Dressed in a granny-style nightgown, the girl held a rag doll and a worn, satin blanket tightly. "My name is Danielle. Will you rock me?" she asked solemnly.

"Of course I will, honey," Melanie answered, immediately bending to pick up the girl and cuddle her. "Would you like me to sing to you, too?"

"My mommy always does," Danielle answered, looking up at Melanie hopefully. "You're pretty. Uncle Sloan is sick. But he's been taking good care of me."

"Oh, I can see that. But now I'm here to take care of both of you," Melanie answered, settling in an oak rocker much too large for her. She began to rock the little girl and hum.

Along the way, she began to think of ways that Sloan could repay her kindness....

Tangled in his bed sheets and running a fever, Sloan awoke to a scent filling the apartment that he decided was ambrosia of potato soup. Danielle whispered quietly in the kitchen and a woman's husky—sultry—voice blended with his niece's.

In a fever, he dreamed of a cool, soft hand scented of flowers resting on his forehead. A soothing feminine voice urged him to drink chilled orange juice. "Danielle is sleeping. You need to rest, too. Go back to sleep. I'll take care of everything."

Sloan closed his eyes. "Thanks, Maxine. I knew I could count on you."

Gentle arms lifted his head to replace the pillows, which had fresh, cool cases.

Struggling to awake later, he stood shakily, placed one foot in front of another and swayed to the bathroom.

When he stepped into the hall again, a small woman—the most beautiful, feminine woman he had ever seen—stood within two feet of him. Framed in the dim light, she paused in midstep. Wide blue eyes, with thick, dark brown lashes, dominated an elfin-shaped face. Masses of golden curls framed her head, catching the dim light like dew on morning grass.

Sloan blinked, then continued his slow inspection of the beautiful nymph captured in time, like a doe in a grassy highland meadow, poised for flight.

The scent of spring flowers swirled around him, a delicate fragrance of roses and daisies.

Soft, romantic music filled the air, and Sloan realized that this small, exquisite creature was formed for him. She would be his other half, his heart's true love.

Entranced, Sloan stared as the tip of the small goddess's tongue slid to moisten her full, pink lips.

A tendril clung to small earlobes that Sloan instinctively knew were unscathed by another man's lips. Her skin resembled warm, creamy silk, and he longed to stroke her flushed cheek with his fingertips.

His T-shirt draped across luscious, pert breasts and traced rounded hips. Without hesitating he reached slowly toward her, placing his hands on a tiny waist.

The woodland nymph's eyes widened, resembling two blue snow lakes.

Taking his time, Sloan framed her small face with his palms. He traced the delicate bones and silky warm flesh with his thumbs, aware that she breathed slowly, as trapped by the moment as he.

He touched a velvety earlobe with the tip of his finger, followed the delicate whorls to ease aside silky curls. Moving slowly, fearing that a sudden move would send the nymph into the mists of eternity, Sloan traced the slender arc of her eyebrow.

Sliding his finger down her cheek, he smiled tenderly at the vision, realizing that he alone had caused her hot blush...a maiden's blush when touched by the man who was destined to have her.

"I've been waiting all my life for you," he said quietly before bending his head slowly.

Her lips tasted of honey and orange ambrosia and smelled of baby powder. She was exactly as Sloan had dreamed.

She inhaled slowly as his hand moved to claim her breast. "How perfect you are, my love," he murmured against her soft, sweet lips.

Her heartbeat caught him, blended with his magically as she answered his kiss timidly.

Her soft breast filled his hand perfectly, and Sloan couldn't resist running his thumb slowly across the poignant hardened tip.

"Sloan..." she whispered in a voice so husky and low that he thought of spring wind sweeping through cool pine boughs. "You should rest . . . go back to bed."

Sloan trembled, checking his need to deepen the kiss. Woodland nymphs could be easily frightened away after all. Fear slammed into his belly—if he slept, the vision could escape and never return. Then Sloan heard himself whisper, "My heart . . . I love you. Come to bed with me. . . . Let me hold you while we sleep."

"Sloan..." she protested on a soft sigh as he bent to pick her up gently, as though she were wafer-thin china.

She fitted into his arms perfectly, a small, soft woman made especially for him.

Taking care, Sloan carried her to his bed. He placed her in the center of a space much too large for her. When he could, Sloan decided dreamily, he would fill their bed with rose petals.

"Sloan, this isn't wise. . . ." she whispered, looking up at him and pulling the sheet up to her chin. "You're not feeling well just now. . . ."

Sloan smiled, understanding her delicate sensibilities. Nymphs trapped at midnight had to be courted gently and sweetly. But for now, he needed to hold her while they slept. In time, she would curl against him, trusting him to explore— Sloan slid into bed, gathering her gently against him. "I know what I want, my love. And I want you near me now. Don't be afraid. I'll take very, very good care of you. Later, when you're not frightened . . ."

He smiled again, nestling his chin on top of her fragrant, soft curls and closing his eyes dreamily. "...we'll make love

and talk about how many children we'll have—maybe on a
farm in Iowa.... I do love you...."

Minutes later, Melanie listened to Sloan's heavy heartbeat, her head riding the slow lift and fall of his chest.

*She had just experienced the most beautiful, romantic
moment of her life—with Sloan Raventhrall!*

She breathed quietly, aware that his hand tenderly, possessively cupped her breast.

*Snuggling with Raventhrall in a tender mood was like
playing with a purring, yet unstable vicious tiger...a hungry tiger.*

Foraging valiantly for reality, Melanie decided to ignore
why her breast lay in Raventhrall's hand. The tender, sweet
wooing kiss of a lover had never really happened. She absolutely denied the moment and the scene. It didn't happen...none of this was happening—

Sloan gathered her closer, running his big hand down the
curves of her body intimately and making deep, pleased
masculine sounds within his throat. He stroked her lightly
from head to toe, testing each soft curve experimentally before moving on.

His fingers slid beneath the shirt, edging it higher as she
swallowed. Unerringly, his hand reclaimed her bare breast
and he sighed, a pleased, dreamy sound.

Melanie closed her eyes, forcing herself to breathe quietly. Awakening a sleeping giant could be dangerous to small
women, she decided. She opted to wait to slip away until he
slept fully. Meanwhile, she was trapped by Sloan's hard
body.

Her ex-husband's body had lacked the physical tone of
Sloan's muscular body. Rick's lean frame sported loose
muscle tone; his lovemaking left her disappointed. After
making modest love, Rick snored like a foghorn as he slept.

Sighing deeply, Sloan nuzzled her hair. Somehow he
found her earlobe and kissed it slowly as though absorbing

the feel and scent of her into him. His teeth scraped the sensitive flesh, and tiny, delicate explosions began pinging deep within Melanie.

Gently, persistently, the tip of his tongue touched her ear, following the whorls slowly as his warm breath flowed across her hot cheek.

Melanie suddenly realized that Sloan's free hand was steadily easing beneath her cotton briefs. One long finger pressed intimately against her....

Swallowing tautly, Melanie sucked in her breath, closed her eyes and tried to breathe slowly.

"I've waited for you all my life," he whispered huskily against her throat. Sloan's warm lips trailed steadily downward to unerringly find the tip of her breast.

Suckling delicately, Sloan nuzzled her flesh. "You're perfect, my love," he murmured drowsily.

Melanie trembled. If she could just wait until he fell asleep....

Desire shot through her as he explored her breasts very slowly, very thoroughly. Delicate cords deep within her reacted instantly by tightening until she ached—Melanie closed her eyelids firmly, trying to control the rocketing delight that she'd never before experienced.

He sighed heavily, as though too tired to pursue what he wanted most in life. Carefully, gently, Sloan Raventhrall—stock-market tiger—lay his head on her breasts, nuzzled her once and fell deeply asleep.

Melanie lay perfectly still, aching and incomplete. Sloan's big hand still claimed her breast, the fingers of his other hand resting between her thighs.

In that moment, Melanie knew without a doubt that Sloan's expertise would be devastating. He would be a possessive, tender lover, demanding all eventually.

She had to keep Sloan Raventhrall, would-be lover, from discovering the romantic moment they had just shared.

* * *

Sloan groaned and rose to check on Danielle. In the hall-way, Melanie Inganforde stood outlined in the hall light, her small body curving beneath the loose folds of his T-shirt. She carried a sleeping Danielle in her arms.

He blinked, trying to understand the scene. M. S. Ingan-forde's breasts thrust at his shirt, peaking delicately as he stared. "Mel?"

"M.S. to you," she returned crisply, edging him aside to carry Danielle into her bedroom. Sloan followed Melanie's shapely backside and tested his fever-hot cheek with his palm. The room slanted as he traced the delicate swaying walk. He frowned. Usually Melanie's business jackets cov-ered her hips as she strode through Standards' hallways.

"What are you doing here?" he asked, following her into Danielle's bedroom. Something nagged at him, though he couldn't pinpoint the problem.

"Saving this poor child. Itty's accounts are on your din-ing room table. Or rather, pieces of his accounts. Really, Raventhrall, you ought to hire someone to clean up this mess. Itty's having a fit. He wants action by this afternoon. It's now two o'clock Friday morning—"

The orange juice he'd managed to sip curdled as he re-membered why Melanie was in his apartment.

"Friday?" Sloan counted backward and groaned about the lost week. "No way in hell," he muttered roughly, then ran his hands through his hair. "He wants to diversify. Sell off and reinvest at a whim. He wants to be advised of every move and he's quirky. Has a brain that never stops darting into possible profit cubbyholes. Has sentimental stuff he doesn't want touched. Balancing his portfolio on a mo-ment's notice is impossible."

Peering down at her, Sloan stared at her face. "What's wrong with you? What's missing?"

"I don't know—"

"Your glasses," he stated. "You're not wearing them."

"So I'm not. I don't wear them every minute."

Sloan stared harder, trying to remember something vaguely familiar about Melanie's face.

"I can see well enough not to bump into walls, Sloan," she stated as a blush rose up her cheeks. "Step aside, would you. Danielle is getting heavy."

His throat ached, and he leaned against the doorway as Melanie tucked Danielle in with a kiss.

He blinked. Danielle looked as sweet as an angel. He swung his aching eyes back to Melanie. "What's wrong with your hair? Why isn't it stiff and spiky?"

She flushed instantly, moving past him. "Really, Sloan. You do wonders for my ego...."

"Have you shrunk lately?" he asked seriously, noting that she barely reached his shoulder.

"I am not wearing my pumps," she returned between her teeth without turning to face him.

The doorbell chimed softly and Sloan groaned, placing his fingers to his temples. "Look. I'll call Itty and—"

Melanie straightened, patted Danielle's neatly combed curls and ordered firmly, "You will not. Not until we talk. You owe me, Raventhrall. Remember?"

The doorbell chimed again and Sloan leveled a scowl at Melanie. He smiled nastily. "Feeling our daily power trip, are we, dear?"

"You asked for my help. I told you it would cost," Melanie answered evenly, not in the least frightened as he glared down at her.

She swept by him, grabbed one of his dress shirts and thrust her arms through the sleeves on her way to the door. "That's probably your friend...El Lobo, isn't it? He's here to check on Danielle and you. He called earlier and seemed surprised that a woman answered. Surely you have scores of...feminine guests."

Scooting a chair next to the door, Melanie stood on it to peer through the peephole. Sloan noted that Melanie's legs were indeed long and feminine. He particularly enjoyed the way his T-shirt rested on her rounded bottom. He frowned, unable to pinpoint why the shape of Melanie's bottom should interest him. Then he decided to ignore the soft, luscious curve, since his vision was probably affected by his fever.

Satisfied with the visitor's identity, she stepped down and drew his shirt firmly around her. "El Lobo himself. Fresh from a date. When I answered your telephone, he insisted on paying a house call, more from curiosity than anything else, I suspect."

She opened the door, and El Lobo stepped into the room, his dimpled, lady-killer grin firmly in place. His eyes slid down Melanie's petite body, which was swathed in the huge folds of Sloan's dress shirt. Sloan frowned as El Lobo's gaze stayed overlong on Melanie's long, slender legs.

The pediatrician began to smirk as he looked at Sloan, who stood leaning against the wall, dressed only in his shorts. Placing his leather bag on the table, El Lobo rolled up his sleeves. "You didn't tell me you'd imported a private nurse, old chap," he said, his leer growing.

"Mel, meet Miles Lobella, pediatrician... Miles, meet Mel. She's here to help me on business." Sloan didn't like El Lobo's slow, calculating appraisal of Melanie's bare legs. "Business, Miles," he said firmly through a sore throat.

"Uh-huh," Miles agreed in a disbelieving tone, sticking a thermometer in Sloan's mouth. He vanished down the hallway to check on Danielle and returned quickly to retrieve the thermometer. He scanned it briefly. "You're running quite a fever, old chum. Ah...didn't interrupt anything that would cause your temperature to rise, did I?"

Sloan's head hurt, sudden unexplained anger surging through him. A small, cool hand touched his cheek, stopping him from moving toward El Lobo, who looked mildly surprised. The hand stroked him gently and Sloan looked into Melanie's blue eyes. Standing between the two tall men, she said quietly, "Back off, El Lobo. Don't pick on Sloan. He isn't feeling well. We're working together on a project that has to be finished tomorrow."

El Lobo's teeth gleamed in his tanned face. "No way. He's dead on his feet."

"Sloan has always been marvelous when he's on a deadline. But now he has me to help him through his trials, don't you, Sloan?"

"Here, take these," Miles said, placing tablets in Sloan's hand. In the next minute, he slapped an "I've been a good boy" sticker on Sloan's forehead and whisked out of the apartment.

Sloan groaned, sprawling into his favorite chair. He searched the cushions, extracted a tiny doll and propped his chin on it. "No way can I put a package together for Itty by this afternoon. Not in this shape."

Melanie took the tablets from Sloan and ordered, "Open." She slipped two tablets onto his tongue, urging him to drink water. "Sloan, don't panic. All you have to do is sign this paper, and I'll manage everything."

"What paper?" Sloan's head throbbed; his throat refused to allow his swallow.

Papers rattled again, the sound cutting at his head like a power drill. "This is a little contract I drew up for our private business arrangement...you'll get a carbon copy. It says that Itty's account will be turned over in its entirety to me, and that in return I'll help you through this catastrophe."

"That's blackmail. Itty would never want a woman handling his account."

"You're going to help me put together a satisfactory package for him and work with me...support me, if you will...until he is my, I repeat, my *un*returnable client."

"Boggles the mind.... Itty would chew you to bits. Working with him requires patience and control...a firm hand. Has buying-and-selling whims you wouldn't believe...." Sloan opened one eye to stare at the paper Melanie rattled before his face.

"I don't think so. Not with you backing me all the way. We'll start by reviewing all the notations—your bits of napkins, paper sacks and notes—and see if I've organized them properly. Then of course, I'll manage Danielle until you recover. Apparently there's a baby-sitting problem."

"Blackmail."

"I know. Isn't it great?" Melanie asked. She slowly peeled away the gold foil "I've been a good boy" sticker from Sloan's forehead, and he groaned again.

"Danielle is staying for two months," he said doggedly, refusing to fall before her siege too easily. "Her parents need a rest, and they're building a new house. They'll be at a collection point sometime at the first of November, unless there's an emergency. My mother took a bus headed west. Jessica's—my sister's—in-laws refused delivery. That left me."

Sloan had the premonition that if he could just hold Melanie, perhaps tangle those cool, slender limbs against his aching hot body, everything in his world would return to normal.

"I'll want another good account, too," Melanie whispered after a moment in which he studied the delicate little strawberry-shaped birthmark on the side of her neck.

"Double blackmail," he grumbled, remembering suddenly that Melanie possessed a greedy, all-business heart.

"Two months of helping with Danielle," she nudged. "Think of it, Sloan...two whole months. Or I walk right now, and you can cope with Itty and Danielle alone."

Three

———

At six o'clock Friday morning, Melanie sat on Sloan's massive bed. Propped up by pillows and surrounded by a clutter of paper and notes, she was thrilled. Sloan dozed restlessly beside her, a washcloth covering his forehead. He awakened with a growling, hibernating bear noise when Melanie nudged him with her elbow. "Mmm. What?"

Melanie smiled benignly, knowing that everything she'd ever wanted was just within her grasp. Riding high with her victory, she decided that sitting upright in Sloan's bed to get his attention as he dozed was a small concession. Allowing her a tiny space, he sprawled across the bed, and his warmth radiated around her companionably. Her briefcase served to separate their spaces. She glanced down Sloan's tanned body and pushed away the slight tingle of awareness racing hotly through her. After all, Sloan's romantic character was an effect of his fever, not his true nature—that of a predatory, insensitive jerk. "Do you think Itty will want to sell off his Apeman Enterprise stock?"

Sloan groaned dramatically. "Don't you ever stop talking? We've been working at Itty's account for hours. If the damn thing isn't taking shape by now, it never will. The sound of you straightening all that paper hurts my head. Stop rocking the bed."

"Of course. You're right...maybe it's time to stop. We've managed to put together a good package for Itty. Now all you have to do is to sign this letter of explanation to Itty. I think we should reel him in slowly, and this letter just says that I'm working in your place, but that you have absolute confidence in my ability. If Itty questions my ability, of course, you'll have to stand firm and say that you're tutoring me on his accounts, and that I am the only person...repeat, only qualified person...that you would entrust with his account."

She could afford to be kind now, Melanie decided as she smiled tenderly. Sloan's signature scrawled across Itty's ownership papers was her security that soon she would be climbing the ladder of success. In the past few hours, she'd siphoned angles and tips from Sloan. He played a whimsical, inventive game, acting on educated intuition rather than ratios and profit margins. When Itty was the game, his advisor had to be ahead of the loser whims and nurture the winners. Occasionally, Sloan had allowed Itty a "baby," an account to foster and pet until it grew into a winner. There were solid judgment decisions at the base of Sloan's thinking, which he apparently did best while he was engaged in a sports activity.

Sloan rolled cautiously toward her. He rested his head on the pillow and stared up at her. His hair stood out in peaks, and a black stubble covered his jaw. Fever tinted his dark skin at the cheekbones; his brown eyes squinted cautiously up at her. He resembled a distraught mountain man hanging over a bottomless canyon and clinging by his fingertips to the roots of a dead brush. "How can you do this to me in good conscience? Isn't taking advantage of me at a time like this a little dishonest?''

Melanie began to neaten and alphabetize the papers and jot down notations. She reached for a stack of napkin bits bearing Sloan's scrawl that rested on his chest. He caught her hand. "Don't you feel the least bit guilty, Mel?''

She shook her head, and Sloan noted how small and delicate her hand was within his. Experimentally, he laced his fingers with hers, fitting the small soft palm against his. Staring at their hands, he reminded her, "I hate it when a woman gloats.... I'm a sick man, Mel.''

When she withdrew her hand quickly, Sloan regretted the loss. "Yes, you are, Sloan," she said. "El Lobo says you could be recovering for two weeks... with someone to help you bear your burdens. That's me, of course, the little burden-bearer. During that time, you can acquaint me with Itty's peculiar tastes. We can talk about another great account for me.''

"How's Danielle?" Sloan didn't want Melanie to move away. He wanted to hold and cuddle her. He wanted *her* to cuddle and hold *him*. He glanced down her legs and leaned closer. M. S. Inganforde reminded him of a woodland sprite at play among her favorite stock-market grasses. "You're not wearing your glasses, Mel.''

"I don't always wear them, Sloan." She scooted off the bed and breezed out of the room. He wistfully noted the soft quiver of flesh beneath his T-shirt and closed his eyes firmly. M. S. Inganforde wasn't a woman, she was a machine gobbling up his empire.

Sloan mulled on that and listened to Melanie talk quietly to Danielle in the kitchen. Then Danielle slid into bed beside him, smelling of her favorite bubble bath. She hugged her cherished doll. "I like Melanie. I'm glad she's going to be taking care of us, Uncle Sloan. She's going to come home at noon and stay with us until you're better. She fixed my favorite cereal and juice for you. Melanie is neat," she whispered sleepily. "She's a mommy lady, but she doesn't have kids."

Sometime later, Sloan dragged his weak body out of bed to check on his former bachelor kingdom. Danielle, propped amid pillows, blankets and dolls, a telephone at her fingertips, dozed in front of a children's television program. The kitchen washer and dryer units chugged and thumped companionably. The dishwasher hummed. He discovered a note, with Melanie's full, loopy handwriting resting exactly on the lines, taped to the refrigerator. *S. Will be back early this afternoon. Danielle will call if problems. Juice in fridge. Soup in slow cooker. Take your pills when you wake up. Thanks for Itty. M.*

"Blackmailer. Pirate," he muttered. Taking two tablets from a childproof bottle, Sloan swallowed them with water and groaned under the weight of his headache. Later he would worry about Itty's wrath; now he wanted a steamy hot shower and bed. M. S. Inganforde would pay dearly for her acts of piracy on the stock-market seas when he was back up to full speed.

Sloan stepped into the bathroom, scowled at the neat arrangement of his shaving supplies and stripped off his shorts. He stepped into the large shower stall, turned on the water and allowed the steam and water to encompass his aching body. He shampooed and rinsed, and soaped his body thoroughly, hoping that somehow Melanie wouldn't foul Itty's portfolio beyond recovery.

Something soft and slippery wet brushed his arm, and Sloan opened his lids to see his nymph swathed only in steam. Backed into a corner, her wet hair coiling around her face, her beautiful wide blue eyes stared helplessly up at him. Incredibly soft and womanly, she shielded her bosom and lower with her hands. Sloan noted her lush curves and tiny waist, savoring the moment when he could truly make her a part of him.

She'd come to rescue him from M. S. Inganforde's clutches.

Her eyes touched his chest, his flat stomach and hips and his... Swelling with desire, Sloan allowed the water to sluice between them, shielding his arousal slightly. When the time was right, she would be less frightened. Nymphs took a fair amount of courting, but he could wait. It was right, somehow, that they should stand unclothed and very much aware of each other. "Hello, sweetling," he whispered, feeling suddenly much better. "I'm so glad you've come to me. Have I told you today how much I love you?"

When she shook her head side to side, Sloan eased her small hand away from her breasts to kiss it. "I do," he whispered, nibbling on the back of her hand and pressing the soft palm to his mouth. "You'll see."

"You're very... large," she whispered huskily over the sound of running water.

"Yes." Sloan lifted her arm to kiss her inner wrist and then her elbow.

Drawing her carefully against him, Sloan closed his eyes, savoring the lush, warm, womanly form he'd ached for all his life. He was complete finally, wrapped in his life-mate's embrace. He'd waited, waded through years, for just this perfect woman. He rested his chin on the top of her head and sighed happily as he stroked her back and rounded bottom. Taking care, he touched the breasts nestled against him, traced their shape lightly as she shivered. "Put your arms around me, sweetheart," Sloan urged softly.

She stiffened, drawing back slightly as his aroused form touched her stomach. "No. You're frightening me, Sloan. You don't feel well... you're not yourself, and I..."

He bent to kiss her mouth, gently inserting his tongue and licking the water from her bottom lip. "I understand, my own dear heart. I can wait."

Turning off the faucets, he tugged a thick bath towel from the top of the stall and dried her gently. He kissed the fragrant flesh he dried, smiling as he knelt to better dry her slender thighs and legs. It was much better to wait, enticing his nymph with bits of lovemaking until she wanted him as badly as he wanted her. "There, my love," he whispered, kissing her soft stomach and each breast. "Step out now and keep warm. Remember I love you and come back to me soon."

"He did what, Peaches?" Itty demanded in Sloan's office later that morning. He widened his legs into a defensive stance and glared down at Melanie. "Sloan knows I don't like getting shafted.... I ended up in the slammer on a bum dime rap—that's ten years, lady—all because I hooked up with somebody who didn't know arson from auto theft. From then on I promised myself that Itty Bitty works only with pros. I came out of the joint squeaky clean, bought new threads and decided to keep myself on the straight and narrow. No broad is going to send me back because of bad investments."

Itty shook his craggy head and continued muttering. "That boy must be sick. Blondes and business.... He knows I don't do business with women. They're undependable, chocked full of moods and whims and such, like my baby— the woman I'm going to marry. But that's okay, she's not the sort to mix business and—" Itty glanced at Melanie and blushed slightly before he continued. "A man's brain is made for business...."

Melanie counted to fifty while she listened to Itty's opinion of the feminine business brain. When Itty paused to stare at the television screen and a home-run hit, Melanie said quietly, "Waymon's batting average is up this year. The Cards have a good chance since the pitcher's left shoulder operation. His curve ball is unbeatable—"

"Yeah. But that shoulder operation has been costing—" Itty's head pivoted toward Melanie. "What do you know about the Cards?"

Melanie made a mental note to study the Cardinals. Perhaps she would organize Sloan's napkin-piece notes on the players. "My favorite team."

"Yeah? What pitcher was a Harlem Globetrotter?"

"Bob Gibson."

"How many home runs did Stan the Man hit?"

"475." Melanie answered a quick succession of questions without error, including what happened to Dizzy Dean's toe.

Itty mulled the idea over, then said, "Raventhrall has been okay in the past. If he's hitting rough times, guess I can work with you—so long as he's pulling the strings and keeping profits up."

Melanie took a deep breath, drew herself up to her full height, and said, "Actually, Itty, Sloan recommended that I take over your account completely. If my work isn't satisfactory when he's better, your account will revert to him."

"Women don't think good when it comes to business," Itty persisted.

"Try me," she said blithely. "I'll get you good seats for the next Cards game."

"I like to play poker now and then while I'm talking business. Only one woman I ever met can play a good game," Itty prodded, leaning over her to intimidate her with a stream of cigar smoke. His craggy face softened mysteriously as he added, "Beautiful woman...real lady...a widow. Gonna marry her if she'll have me. Great little homemaker, dynamite with cards and great in the s—" He glanced warily at Melanie and dropped his last word back into his barrel chest.

Melanie held her breath, opened Sloan's desk drawer and drew out an unopened deck of cards. "We can work together mornings. Five-card draw?" she asked.

"Damn," Itty said quietly, taking off his suit jacket and sitting down to shuffle the cards.

Twenty minutes later, he groaned, pitched his cards on the table and stared at her blankly. "Bluffed me with a full house. Only one other woman I know plays like that." He shook his head and ordered, "Cut 'em, kid."

An hour later Itty growled a satisfied noise, puffed on his cigar and ordered her to take action, acquiring Mogul Enterprises securities.

When Itty chugged out of the office, Melanie sat back in Sloan's massive chair, neatly stacked the poker deck and slid it into a box. She methodically made the necessary calls, notes to the files, and logged into Standards' computer banks. Then behind closed doors, she spun around twice in the chair and laughed with delight.

Rivulets of rain ran down the smoked-glass window, and Melanie smirked as she savored her victory with Itty and the promises of the future. It had been years since she'd gotten to smirk wickedly and reveled in it now.

Devereau strode past Sloan's office without stopping to chat, as he normally did with his star player. Once again she had been overlooked, and she decided to drop smirking, for now. Melanie glanced at the telephone notes waiting for Sloan's return. Mimi, Traci, Lori, LaBelle and other amazons were getting desperate on a diet without Sloan. Melanie frowned as she thought of Sloan's latent romantic tendencies.

He could be devastating, charming and lovable. But the tender lover wasn't the Sloan she knew quite well. Sloan was not patient, adoring, nor loving. Sloan was dynamic, with the instincts of a shark.

This morning, she'd just finished her shower when Sloan came in for his, and she'd almost melted into his arms. In her lifetime, she'd never been—she hunted for the right term—supped like a blend of ambrosia and honey. Or tasted, like a goddess meant for Sloan's touch alone.

She'd never had a man smile at her so tenderly, so lovingly. Sloan—the lover—had been totally absorbed in discovering and protecting her. In those indescribable moments, she knew that Sloan had never revealed his sensitive-lover side to another woman.

The thought was devastating. She'd seen him in action with members of his amazon team. Sloan treated women with an offhand, this-is-the-way-I-am carelessness. His efforts to pursue and beguile were not bestowed with the same concentration as he had given Melanie.

Could his fever have created a dual personality? she wondered.

Melanie frowned, aware of the new, taut aching that had developed in her body. Perhaps it had something to do with the way Sloan's hair-roughened chest had pressed against her... or the way he nibbled at the tips of her breasts until she ached for him to...

She swallowed, reached for a cup of hot water and drank it hastily.

The liquid searing her throat did not dislodge the way Sloan—the lover—could affect her... make her heart race and her bones liquefy. Sloan was a very, very sexy man in his aroused state. His large hands had trembled as they moved gently, expertly over her. He had touched her body as if committing it to memory, loving every inch.

Then, of course, his arousal had pressed against her strongly. It stated, quite elegantly, that at some point, there would be tropical storms and heat waves before the pink mist drifted over them.

Melanie shivered beneath her gray pinstriped suit. *She must never let Sloan know how his romantic nature affected her.*

Saturday midmorning, Sloan struggled weakly over the miles of carpeting to the living room. He braced his hand against the wall, frowned, then peeled away a large foil star pasted on his forehead. Apparently El Lobo had struck again.

Sloan scowled at his usurped kingdom and the vacuum cleaner roaring across his carpet. Dressed in a baggy sweatshirt and tight, worn jeans, Melanie clicked off the metal noise-making monster and smiled at him. "Feeling better? You should have some breakfast...or beef and barley soup."

Danielle looked up from stacking magazines and grinned as she ran toward him. "Uncle Sloan. Horsey...play horsey."

Swallowed by fear, Sloan took a step backward just as Melanie reached down neatly and scooped Danielle into her arms. She kissed the girl's cheek and whispered, "Remember, Danielle. Uncle Sloan isn't feeling well. We must be very careful with him...."

Sloan closed his eyes, trying to remember the words swirling around him. Eons ago he'd promised a woman he'd be very careful with her— He stared at Melanie as she whisked Danielle into the kitchen. "We're making cookies, Sloan...a family recipe. Why don't you eat something while you watch?"

He looked at the apartment and scowled. "You're cleaning. You'll put things away in the wrong places. Do you have to putter every waking moment?" he demanded. "Someone out here was beating a spoon against a pan, doing a mile a minute. Sounded like a damn helicopter back in the bedroom."

Melanie placed a bowl of steaming soup on the table. "Stop growling. It's a pretty day outside. Danielle and I are making cookies, then we're going for a short walk. By the way, I've left your telephone number on my mother's answering machine. I'm expecting her any day now."

"Danielle has been sick—she can't go outside. She'll have a relapse. My sister will kill me. So will my mother," Sloan muttered darkly as he padded over to sit slowly at the table. The rich beef barley soup did look inviting.

"Fresh air will do her good. Just remember not to worry when you wake up and we're gone. El Lobo says you need plenty of rest...that you've been...working hard, and your resistance to this flu is down.''

"You're in cahoots with that fiend from Bottle and Diaper Alley," Sloan returned, sipping the beefy broth. He didn't like El Lobo prowling around his lair...and he didn't understand the hair at the back of his neck rising when he thought of Melanie fending off the pediatrician's well-practiced advances. "The lady shark and the lady-killer. Quite a combo.''

Danielle hugged him, and Sloan returned the favor, noting her neat braids and clean face. "Melanie and me is going to take very good care of you, Uncle Sloan.'' She patted his beard sympathetically. "We can play horsey when you're feeling better, okay? Melanie and me is going to shop for your robe when I feel better. Melanie and me is going to make cookies.''

Sloan glared at Melanie's bland face. "I don't need a robe.... What's wrong with my shorts? They're cotton and virginal.''

Wide-eyed, Danielle leaned against him. "What's a virginal, Uncle Sloan?''

Sloan took a deep breath and watched Melanie smirk. "Stock-market term . . . I'll explain when you're thirty.''

Changing expressions slowly, Melanie pushed her lips into a kind smile, one that showed her even teeth. "Feminine sensibilities, Sloan. I am spending time here until you recover a bit more to take charge of Danielle, remember? We agreed. Danielle should be respected, too.''

"Don't change things, Inganforde," he threatened, sipping his soup. "I like everything just the way it was.''

"Uh-huh.'' She swept past him to begin unloading the dishwasher. Danielle concentrated on placing the forks and spoons in the drawer's correct divider. Sloan stared at the two females clucking over his ruined kingdom and promised revenge when his body was willing.

"What about Itty?" he asked, wondering if his legs would carry him back to his bed.

His gaze snagged on Melanie's taut jeans. There was something familiar about the rounded shape of her bottom.... She reached high to replace dishes, and Sloan wiped away the perspiration beading his upper lip. If she were any woman but a career-hungry...

He thought of resting his aching head on Inganforde's hard businesswoman's chest and closed his lids as he groaned. *He wanted his kingdom back. He wanted Itty's account back. He wanted Inganforde barred from his life.*

Safely tucked in bed later, Sloan placed his arms behind his head and concentrated on remembering something sweet and soft and lovable that had touched him recently.... But his headache grew, and he rolled to one side, aware that he had signed away his fate to a woman who washed dishes and put them away immediately after a meal. Who managed a tyrannical niece as though she were a sweet, lovable child....

Inganforde was damn well taking over his life.

Sloan awoke to Itty's bawdy laughter and Danielle's giggles. Rolling his head slowly to view his bedside clock, he discovered it was 8:00 p.m. He poured a glass of ice water from the thermal jug near his bed, sipped it slowly and waited for the bad dream to evaporate.

Itty's laughter blended with a rippling sound of feminine delight. Prying himself off his bed, Sloan walked down the long hallway to find El Lobo, Danielle, Itty and Melanie playing cards and eating popcorn. Melanie laughed outright, scooped the poker chips toward her and stacked them neatly. Sloan stared at her; no one in his experience made stacks and lines of two chips. El Lobo said something and she laughed again. The delighted female sound, low and husky, a very sexy sound, belonged to Melanie—M. S. Inganforde.

Shaking his head, the defeated warrior struggled back to his bedroom and quietly, firmly, closed his door. In a defiant gesture, he slid out of his shorts before lying down.

Aeons later, Sloan awoke to the sound of delicate sobbing. He lay listening for a time, then rose, padding toward the heartbreaking sounds of a woman in distress. Passing the linen closet, he reached for a towel and wrapped it around his hips.

There in front of his television, curled on his large sectional couch, was his ladylove. He smiled tenderly, realizing that she had been watching a heartrending classic movie.

The soft light coming from the screen outlined his lifemate's curling hair, touching her delicate features as he watched from the shadows. Tears brimmed from her misty eyes, clung to her lashes and trailed down her cheeks.

Dressed in a flowing, silky gown that clung to her voluptuous curves, revealing and concealing, his ladylove waited for him to comfort her. She hugged a throw pillow to her soft bosom, and Sloan knew that, in time, she would be holding him as closely.

It was nice to be needed, Sloan decided tenderly. A truly feminine woman waiting for him alone to tend her needs.

He smiled whimsically. She needed his child in her arms, nursing at her breasts.

But not quite yet. Not until they had supped from passion's table and taken their fill.

Then there would be time for raising their children, born of their love—perhaps on that farm in Iowa.

Startled as he stroked her hair, she stared up at him, her eyes wide. "Sloan! You should be resting...."

He brushed his finger down her cheek, drying it and tasting the tear's salt on his flesh. "How can I sleep away from you, my love?" he asked, easing to the couch to lift her onto his lap.

She was stiff in his arms, but he understood and waited for her to relax. Stroking her back gently, he propped his chin on her bare shoulder, kissed its silky slope as he watched the screen, and whispered, "I love this movie, too."

It was important to Sloan that his ladylove knew they shared the same interests. He wanted her absolutely comfortable to reveal her emotions to him.

Because when the time was right, Sloan wanted her to be absolutely, completely unashamed of her love and passion for him. Their lovemaking would be perfect....

He kissed her bare shoulder, easing the thin strap aside with his teeth. "Sloan..." she protested, huskily, breathlessly, and he smiled, rubbing his lips along her throat.

"Relax...just let me hold you, my love," he urged in a whisper as he found her delicate earlobe.

"You're not well...." she managed shakily after taking a long, uneven breath. She squirmed slightly, and Sloan closed his eyes as desire filled him. She was so soft, so sweet, her hips fitting exactly across his lap. He tried not to tremble, staying the need to push her too quickly.

"I'm much better. I've waited for you...." He breathed unevenly as the tense heat rose between them. Taking care, Sloan eased aside his towel while his other hand found her silk-covered breast. She responded so sweetly to his touch, sighing and trembling, as he caressed the soft shape. Easing his hand to touch her other breast, Sloan nibbled on her throat, kissing the tiny strawberry-shaped birthmark.

"Oh, Sloan...we shouldn't...." she protested huskily, whimsically. He caught the note of yearning, and smiled down at her gently.

"Maybe not...but then maybe we should," he returned, easing his hand beneath her gown to find her soft thighs.

They were slender, soft, strong beneath his exploring fingers. Perfect womanly thighs meant for cradling.... Sloan trembled, unable to hide his need. "Don't be frightened," he whispered huskily. "It's only natural that we should want to make love. I've waited so long for you that waiting longer is agony. But for now, I just want to touch and hold you. Then, when the time is right, you'll want me, too."

She trembled wildly as he found her moist heat with his fingertips, gliding easily over her skin. Her arms encircled his neck tightly, clinging to him as they kissed.

She was everything—heat, wind, fire. An explosion that ignited every sensual, masculine sense within Sloan. She returned his kiss with a hunger that startled him at first.

When she tugged him closer, Sloan hesitated. Her fingers tightened on his shoulders as they stared into each other's eyes, and from the flickering light of the television, the stars pledged undying love. "You complete me," Sloan whispered against her sweet lips. "My other half, my life's mate, my love."

"Oh . . . Sloan," she returned in a broken whisper. "You can be so . . . romantic."

"Only with you, my dove, my fair, sweet peach. . . ." He lifted the gown from her in one swift movement, laid her down tenderly on the cushions and feasted his eyes upon her lush body.

To take her too quickly would spoil the ultimate passion Sloan knew they would share. He sought instead to explore and build her passion over a time until the moment was ripe. He wanted her to remember all their lives the first time he claimed her, the ultimate passion that would seal their lives together.

She'd look wonderful in a white, flowing gown, a path of flower petals leading her to the church altar, him and their marriage vows.

Gently caressing her pale body with a slow sweep of his hand, Sloan leaned down to nuzzle her breasts and taste her silky flesh. She smelled of flowers and woman and future—hot, melting passion. . . . "Oh . . . oh . . . Sloan," she sighed, trembling as his hand claimed her perfect, creamy breast and he bent to taste the ripe tip.

The explosions went rippling through her, surprising him until he remembered how she lacked experience. Laying his cheek over her rapid heartbeat, Sloan used every dram of his self-control as he stroked and comforted her.

Gradually she stopped trembling, and Sloan kissed her tenderly. "You see? Everything is going to be perfect when the time is right. For now, let me see you to your room, my ladylove."

Wondering vaguely why he was so weak, Sloan lifted his nymph into his arms and carried her to her bedroom door. Placing her carefully on her feet, he lifted her chin with the tip of his finger to kiss her lips. "Soon," he whispered, noting with satisfaction how her long lashes closed when he kissed her. How her warm lips clung to his. "Soon, my love. I think it's time I began looking for a proper wedding ring, don't you? Tell me, would you like a farmhouse in Iowa?"

Four

Melanie retrieved the Sunday morning paper from the front door of Sloan's apartment. Floating on a romantic, yet confusing cloud and glowing with a man's loving caress was a new experience for her. She'd placed the filled sugar bowl in the dishwasher and her cup of hot water in the refrigerator.

To keep Sloan from discovering the identity of his dream lover, Melanie had sprayed and spiked her hair.

She returned to the kitchen and Danielle, who was neatly stacking the remnants of her paper-doll handiwork. Danielle—once limits and schedules were defined—was an exceptionally lovable child. Like Itty, she could be handled, but the trick was to be ahead of the inquisitive brain.

Her Uncle Sloan, on the other hand, knew how to love a woman until she melted. Or flamed. Melanie had awakened at dawn with a start, remembering Sloan's towel and her gown intimately tangled at the base of the couch. Creeping out to recover the evidence, she had noted the two tiny, broken straps and frowned. Apparently Sloan's big hands were not truly gentle... though when he touched her body, his hands were beautiful, loverlike.

Some dark, denied feminine particle of Melanie wished that she could spend the rainy, quiet morning snuggling next to Sloan's warm, hard body.

Melanie ached to explore the outer edges of steamy lovemaking that Sloan had awakened in her... to itemize the sensitive points on Sloan and use them to her advantage... their mutual advantage.

She sighed wistfully for a time that would never come. Sloan must never, never know the extent to which his dual personality had affected her, firing her latent... needs.

While Danielle dressed her various paper dolls and chatted with them, occasionally asking advice, Melanie sipped hot water and tried to concentrate on her work. Sloan slept quietly until ten o'clock when she opened his bedroom door. Melanie carefully eased the breakfast tray into Sloan's dark lair.

The tang of woodsy soap, and a dark menacing nuance that she identified cautiously as Sloan's particular male scent, engulfed her. She paused in midstep, aware of her flesh tightening over her body. Aware of how her nerves instantly alerted to the presence of the man who had tenderly introduced her to her first shattering, sensual explosion.

The wedge of light from the hallway sliced into the darkness as she stepped farther into Sloan's room.

"Shut the damn door, Mel," Sloan ordered in a dangerous, bearlike growl.

She raised her eyebrows. Apparently Sloan-the-lover had disappeared.

Sloan-the-ill-tempered lay propped up on pillows, his arms crossed over his chest. A kingsize pillow lay intimately against his side, giving the impression it had been well hugged. A sheet lay low on his stomach, the white cotton contrasting with the tanned, hairy skin above it. Melanie noted that he had shaved, evidenced by three pieces of toilet paper attached to his jaw. She didn't like the set of that jaw. Nor the muscle flexing impatiently over it.

He smiled nastily as she approached. "Having fun stacking and cleaning? That blasted feather duster scrapes when you dust. Sound carries, you know. I heard everything. I've been lying in here awake for hours, hoping you'd find someone else to torture."

"You make me feel so wanted. You were sound asleep, at least until an hour ago. I checked," she said, smiling as she eased the breakfast tray toward Sloan's lap.

"I had a restless night. Up and down. Sits hard on a man when a woman uses him," Sloan muttered.

"Uses?"

"Taking my best account. Blackmailing me in my time of need. A good Samaritan you aren't, Mel."

"To the victor belongs the spoils, old chum," she returned easily, at once comfortable with Sloan's nasty temper and lowering the breakfast tray to him. She paused in midmotion, discovering a distinctive male shape beneath the cotton covering Sloan's hips. Tiny little pings began deep within her. Little cords began to ache.

He glared at her, taking the tray and placing it over his hips. "Coffee. Black. Now," he muttered, scanning the orange juice, sliced peaches and oatmeal she had prepared. He stared at her blankly for a full second and a half, then frowned.

The hair on the back of her neck lifted slightly. Sloan's expression was that of a man trying to remember something....

His dark brown eyes carefully traced her face, then slid down to pin her breasts beneath the heavy sweatshirt. Melanie eased her shoulders into a slump as he considered the area of her chest. Her specially modified bra minimized her endowments, a concession she had learned in the business world, just as tailored girdles modified her flaring hips.

Endowed petite blondes were not usually taken seriously in business, she had discovered at an early age. The undergarments, sewn by a lingerie seamstress experienced in special needs, allowed her business suits to hang perfectly—loose and serious.

Sloan shook his head slightly as though answering his own questions. "Coffee . . . now," he repeated, downing the orange juice.

"It will cost," she returned, smiling. "Itty wants to buy into Amalgamated Flooring, a tiny company propped up by big family money and used as a tax write-off. He says the manager shared his cell—"

Sloan closed his eyes, leaned back on the pillow wearily as though he willed the business world into another century. "Uh-huh. He tried that on me. He sees you as a pushover. Don't let him get involved. Jump out there and snag something really enticing and challenging. Try something with soya beans or peanuts in the health field. Head him off. Maybe get his friend a job with a profitable company."

He sighed tiredly, his lids opening slightly as he turned to stare at the rain. Wrapped in his thoughts, Sloan lovingly stroked the pillow tucked against his side. The distinct flow of his hand outlined a luscious female body.

Melanie shivered, trying to steady her nerves and heartbeat. Sloan's fingers slid to the pillow and slowly caressed the shape of a female breast, just as he had caressed her.

In the dim light, Sloan's hard face bore a lonely, wistful expression. Was it possible that he longed for the woman of his fevers—herself?

Melanie swallowed hard, caught by the way his large hand slid to touch another pillow-breast.

Her nipples hardened instantly, straining against the heavy confines of her bra. Shocked by the reaction of her body, Melanie tried to steady her hands, locking her fingers behind her. The gesture only served to press her taut breasts against the sweatshirt, defining them. She slumped a little, unwrapped her fingers and swooped to pick up the tray.

Sloan's arousal hadn't diminished. He sighed again, a low wistful purring sound as he traced a rounded pillow-hip. Melanie stared helplessly, her fingers just inches from his body.

Then, as though remembering her presence, Sloan turned to her. His expression was infinitely sad and very tired. "How's Danielle doing?"

Melanie tried to steady her voice. "Better," she managed huskily.

Tensing at once, Sloan gave the impression of a hunter fixed on prey as he flipped over toward her. "Say that again," he demanded, his eyes instantly gleaming as he grabbed her wrist, staying her. His thumb stroked her inner wrist, his fingers completely, possessively circling her fine bones. "Say it just the way you did before."

Realizing that she'd allowed her normal voice to seep into the clipped business tones she'd practiced, Melanie cleared her throat. She strove for the practiced, jaunty tones, business as usual. "Much better. She's cutting out paper dolls and waiting to play horsey."

Sloan stared at her for a second, closed his eyes and frowned. His hand slid away listlessly and returned to possessively claim the pillow. He tugged it under his chin and curled around it, watching the rain hit the windows.

"Ah . . . Sloan, are you all right?" she asked after a moment in which he totally ignored her. "Are you feeling worse?" She'd heard of recovering patients struck by deep depression, and the thought that Sloan could be aching, alone and unloved somehow made her want to hold him close.

Melanie shuddered. Sloan Raventhrall was not a man to hold close and cuddle. She eased from the room, shaken by the emotion racing through her.

Danielle occupied the next few hours, and when she settled down to nap, Melanie was forced to check on Sloan.

She'd been avoiding the moment. Balancing the lap tray, which held juice, her special barley stew and homemade whole-wheat rolls with butter, Melanie eased into the room. This time, she would let him lift the tray....

Sloan lay curled around his pillow, dozing. As though he sensed her changing his water carafe and placing the tray beside the bed, he sighed and asked, "How is Danielle?"

"Fine. She's napping."

He sighed deeply, held the pillow possessively in the crook of his arm and asked wistfully, "Have you ever been in love, Mel?"

Striving for a light note, Melanie said, "Hundreds of times."

He breathed deeply once and turned slowly. Melanie ached when she saw tired lines etched around Sloan's eyes. He gave the appearance of a man haunted by memories. "Sit down, Mel."

When she hesitated, Sloan scowled up at her. "Hell, Mel. Give me credit. I'm just asking for a little adult conversation." He eased aside the assorted teddy bears and dolls Danielle had propped near him for company. "Here. Sit down. You've got my best account, the least you can do is talk to a sick man on his deathbed."

He reached for the tray and placed it over his lap. "You've been nagging me to eat, so talk to me in exchange. Sit."

Melanie snatched a large teddy bear for emotional support and hugged it against her as she perched on the edge of Sloan's bed.

"Have you ever been in love?" he repeated, sniffing her barley stew appreciatively and lifting a spoon to sample it. He studied the rich beef broth laden with carrots, celery and onions.

"Of course. I've loved," she returned defensively. "And been loved. I'm a grown woman, after all, Sloan," she added firmly.

Sloan glanced at her, mocking her use of "grown." "This is good," he murmured after sampling her family soup recipe. "You've been married, right? So have I.... You must have loved enough to marry the guy. Or was it to advance your career? Why did you divorce him?"

Suddenly uncomfortable with revealing her past with Sloan, Melanie held the bear tighter. Sloan explored the ingredients of the soup with interest, snagged a spoonful of barley and watched her expectantly as he ate.

She stared back at him, anger rising. "Darned if I'll spill my private life like pearls before the swine—"

"Chauvinist pig, is the term," Sloan corrected undaunted and licked a buttered crumb from his lips. "Give."

"You were married?" she asked after debating the situation and watching him eat dutifully.

"Worst time of my life. Lasted two years in my pre-thirty era. The final kiss-off came when I lost a promotion to a best friend and found out that she—Eve—couldn't cope with failure. Or anything but a perfect, well-organized life...."

Melanie gnawed on the picture, then said, "So that's why you fight organization."

"Maybe.... Okay, you're wondering, it's written all over you. Sex wasn't that great with Eve. The mechanics were all there—the bodies—but the music and magic just didn't zing. Like a volcano with no lava."

"Zing? Lava?"

Nodding slowly, he answered after sipping his juice. "Zing. As in, Eve didn't really need *me*," Sloan answered, sipping his juice. "Need me in a way that no other man would satisfy," he stated with conviction. "Don't ask me now, or if I'm going nuts, but I just lately discovered the difference," he added in a soft, hollow tone a moment later.

"A woman who needs you has a certain pulse, you know, Mel? And when you touch her, stroke her essence, she...melts. Does wonderful things for the old ego. Makes a man want to cherish and...make old-fashioned love to her from head to toe. He starts seeing images of her dressed as a bride, bearing his child, all the great old-time, American apple-pie stuff."

A premonition that fate was clawing at her doorstep, held at bay by a few ticks of the clock, swept over Melanie. In his illness, Sloan ached for his dream lover.

Sloan continued to talk drowsily when she removed the empty tray and placed it on his bedside table. "Men have needs, Mel," he said, caressing the pillow with long, skillful fingers. "It takes a certain kind of woman to bring them out. You don't understand, but when a woman feels like hot silk...I can't even think about her without getting worked up."

He glanced sleepily at her and settled lower in his bed, nestling his chin firmly over the pillow and drawing it into the spoon of his body. "She smells like flowers and under that, there's this woman fragrance that drives me insane.... She...throbs when I make love to her and the noises—the purring sounds—she makes...I can't imagine what it would be like to fit inside her, pour myself into her.... Incredible.... I want her so much, Mel.... I'm going to find her again, and when I do, I'm never letting go again."

With that, Sloan drifted cozily off into his dreams, leaving Melanie devastated and perspiring. She realized she hadn't breathed, her lungs aching. Her muscles and bones refused to move, forcing her to sit still. Her knuckles ached from choking the teddy bear.

Worst of all, she wanted to slip into Sloan's bed, comfort his aching heart!

Then she wanted everything, just the way he had explained it!

Melanie closed her lids, firmly wiped the back of her hand across the perspiration beading her forehead and stared down at Sloan.

He smiled tenderly in his sleep, cradling the pillow against himself and caressing it gently. "Soon, my darling. Soon...." he whispered lovingly as he nuzzled the pillow.

By the end of the first week, Melanie had resystemized Sloan's apartment. She received a brief note from her mother saying that she would arrive shortly, but wanted to visit a friend for a few days. Delilah had promised to call just as soon as she finalized her plans to visit Melanie.

Though the height of the fever had passed, Sloan required rest and help with Danielle, who clearly idolized Melanie. He resented his weakness, yet awoke with a tremendous urge to make love.

To salvage his star rating at Standards and to demonstrate to Melanie that he always did his share in a disaster, Sloan helped with her work load when he could. It grated that Melanie's small hands were tending his accounts and hers. He began to hate El Lobo's infiltration into the apartment, the happy stickers pasted everywhere like big Zorro signatures.

Maxine refused to return until Danielle vacated the premises. However, she did purchase groceries and run errands for Melanie, reminding Sloan that he had "found an angel in disguise.... No other woman could control 'the demon.'" According to Maxine, M. S. Inganforde was a real woman, the old-fashioned kind who cooked real food and needed a family to tend.

Monday through Friday mornings, M. S. Inganforde baked wonderful whole-wheat rolls formed from an enormous plastic tub kept in the refrigerator. Then she packed Danielle off for a morning at Beck and Call's day nursery.

Devereau, to help his star player recover, allowed Melanie to work in the office during the mornings. Afternoons and evenings, she brought a portable computer and a stuffed briefcase to Sloan's apartment.

Late Friday afternoon, Sloan awoke to the delicious aroma of food. He groaned, hugged his favorite pillow closer and nestled in the flowery scents of the freshly laundered case. Then, after a longing sigh, he struggled to sit and tugged on the bottom half of his sweat suit, his concession to the females infesting his apartment.

Melanie and Danielle were dancing to James Brown music in the kitchen. Sloan stared at the females blankly, then decided to ignore them. He preferred to think of himself as a lion lording royally over his kingdom and ignoring whatever did not touch him. He lay back on the couch, tugged Danielle's favorite satin doll blanket up to his chest and watched the television's stock-market report without interest.

His dream lover hadn't returned, probably frightened off by M. S. Inganforde's small iron hand. Primed for success, she showed no evidence of tiring. Sloan sincerely hated her strength and enthusiasm for working late into the night after Danielle slept.

Danielle stroked his cheek comfortingly. "You're doing better, Uncle Sloan. Uncle El Lobo said that you'll be back to normal in another week of rest. He's counting the days until he can ask Melanie out for dinner. He says she's just the right size to slow dance with."

"That's nice, Danielle," Sloan murmured, vaguely wondering what El Lobo saw in Melanie. She wasn't his type at all. But then, El Lobo's tastes were often unknown. Maybe an all-business female organizer thrilled his pediatrician bones.

He noted dully that Amalgamated Flooring stock had risen a full quarter from the previous report. Listlessly, Sloan asked, "What's she cooking, Danielle?"

"Roast beef with juice. Tomorrow morning is Saturday and Melanie said that's when we can bake bread. Melanie says homemade bread is better for you. Melanie uses natural stuff in it, and she brought me a special jar of home-made jam.''

"Boy, I'm thrilled," Sloan murmured, then yawned hugely. "What's she doing now?"

"Getting ready to play office. Melanie bought me a new coloring book. She bought you one, too. She's says you're under…stress. We're going to play office for one quiet hour. Then I can set the table. Today I got to iron dinner napkins with Melanie's travel iron. Won't playing office be fun, Uncle Sloan?" Danielle's childish voice rose in excitement.

"Great." Sloan strained for an element of pleasure in his tone and cuddled the baby doll Danielle had carefully placed in the crook of his arm. He shifted for comfort, and the doll wet on him. Life in the sick lane did not always pass smoothly, he decided as Melanie came to smirk over him.

The television light struck the peaks in her hair and out-lined her rather uncurved body. Sloan frowned. There was something different about her hips. He distinctly remem-bered a little more fullness.

He sighed, too tired to debate Inganforde's shapeless-bratwurst body beneath the bulky sweatsuit.

"Coming to the table, Sloan?" she asked. "Or do you want your roast beef au jus served on a tray here?"

"I hate your cheerful voice, Mel," Sloan murmured, dragging himself upward and standing as a surge of weak-ness plowed over him.

"Tsk, tsk. Invalidship does not wear well on my liege lord, Raventhrall," she returned happily.

He glared down at her, and then, to recover his pride, he reached out to pat her peaked hair. Melanie danced aside, carefully tugged the peaks upward and glared up at him. Her eyes crackled with anger behind her lenses. "You know I hate it when you do that."

Sloan showed his teeth, and braced with that measure of revenge, decided to work at the computer occupying the dining table. "Did you bring my files?" he asked, easing onto a chair and staring at the neat stacks of accounts with M. S. Inganforde notes dutifully attached.

He tried to concentrate while Danielle colored patiently beside him. "How did you manage this, Mel?" he asked finally, leaning back. "This 'playing office' thing."

She looked over the top of her glasses. "You wouldn't understand. It's an organized effort. There's a right time for everything. Play, then work. Work, then play. Once you set up a workable schedule everything is easy."

"I hate schedules," he returned firmly and inhaled the parfum de roast beef au jus.

The weekend passed, and Sloan managed heroically in the bedroom while another poker game raged in his kitchen.

He spent long hours waiting for his life-mate to come. He needed to cuddle her close. To hear her soft, sexy, wispy voice utter his name in ecstasy.

She never did, though at times a flowery scent floated through the air.

Sloan was truly lonely for the first time in his life. He began listening to the radio beside his bed, preferring romantic music. He also realized how he detested organized businesswomen like M. S. Inganforde. Women should be soft and cuddly, warm welcoming creatures, not methodical list-makers, constantly reading the *Wall Street Journal*.

"You're crabby," she said firmly Sunday night as she prepared to return to her own apartment. "I'll come by after work and stay until Danielle is asleep. We'll work on catching up your work load.... Remember to take Danielle to Beck and Call at promptly eight o'clock in the morning. Devereau says that he doesn't want you overtaxed, and that you are to leave work at noon. He's afraid you'll catch pneumonia just when the stock market is beginning to improve. Just don't forget that Itty is all mine." She smirked widely. "He likes me now. He's in love, you know."

"Bah, humbug," Sloan muttered, quietly slamming the door after her. Then he stripped off his T-shirt and tossed it onto the couch. He studied the homey touch to the neat apartment.

"Everything in its place. There's a time and place for everything," Danielle chirped beside him as she retrieved the T-shirt and handed it to him.

"Fish entrails," he returned darkly.

"Something is wrong with Raventhrall," Devereau whispered as he entered Melanie's small office.

"He's recovering. Working half days was a stroke of genius on your part," Melanie said. Devereau had listened to her suggestion without interest, then the fifth time, he picked up the idea and made it his.

"Mmm. Maybe. Maybe not. I've seen men like him change, forget their true reason for being businessmen. Raventhrall was the best until his flu." Devereau glanced at Sloan as he passed, and ventured happily, "Market is holding steady, eh, Raventhrall? Ready to lock on to those profits and free up the losses?"

Sloan nodded and forced a tight smile. "Benders' LikeMom Soups are up. Beef is holding steady. Pork bellies are the same. Pays to diversify your portfolio."

Devereau cleared his throat. "Anything I can do for you, boy? M.S. could return the Itty account, if it would make you feel better."

Shaking his head, Sloan said, "She's doing fine."

"Anything else troubling you, Raventhrall? You don't seem with the old ball game."

"I'm fine," Sloan returned with a yawn. "Mel has been helping me catch up."

Devereau looked after Sloan as he entered his office. "Something is badly wrong in Raventhrall's life. Find out what it is, Inganforde. Then fix it. I want my star back in fighting shape."

The next day, Mazie Duggins wiggled her latex skirt into Melanie's office. "Everyone is talking about Sloan," she said in a little-girl voice that contrasted with her sexy image. "He's just so...lifeless." She leaned closer to Melanie and whispered secretively, "Sometimes when men get sick, they...uh...you know...lose it."

Melanie shivered, remembering that Sloan hadn't "lost it." He gave every evidence of a man caught in the throes of loneliness. When she entered his office, she found him looking at the bright fall sunlight. The wind tossed fiery oak leaves against the window, and Sloan sighed. "Have you ever just laid in the park and talked with your lover, Mel? Maybe shared a blanket and snuggled in the fallen maple leaves? Winter is coming...snowbound cabins and toasty fires, long cold nights and walks through the snow. I've never made love in front of a blazing fire on a cold winter night. Or in an old-fashioned four-poster bed under a patchwork quilt."

He glanced at her and smiled wistfully. "Of course, you're probably not interested in things like that—the old career doesn't allow much time for smelling the roses, does it? Has your mother called, saying when she'll arrive?"

"She's going to visit a friend first, then she'll call," Melanie answered. Then he sighed again, and Melanie excused herself to walk out of his office on shaky legs.

At the apartment, Sloan tried to concentrate on work, gave up and began coloring with Danielle. He was truly a shell of his former self. A man waiting for his love to reappear. He began watching long, romantic movies and coached Clark Gable through loving Scarlett. After another movie's intense romantic scenes, he dropped to the carpeting and began a fast series of push-ups.

Melanie dreamed of Sloan's expert lovemaking, remembering his expression while tenderly staring down at her body.

She ached for Sloan's erotic lovemaking. For the kisses that melted and heated and the hands that...

Tuesday morning, she walked into Sloan's office carrying her notations on a takeover for a garden-center chain.

Facing the sunshine spread across Kansas City, Sloan patiently snipped the thorns from the welcome-back roses on his desk. A small heap of thorns lay across the unopened sports section of his newspaper. "What are you doing, Sloan?" she asked cautiously, wondering if perhaps the illness had affected him seriously.

"Practicing," he said calmly, distantly. Sweeping a dethorned rose across his cheek, he sighed, inhaling the fragrance and closing his eyes dreamily. "You're not a romantic, Mel. I wouldn't want my sweetheart hurt by thorns. A man never gives his true love roses with thorns."

He sighed again whimsically and brushed the rose petals across his lips, dismissing her.

The middle of the third week, rain pounded Kansas City in gray sheets. The weather matched Melanie's mood. Sloan had lost weight, coming to work looking haggard and worn. Devereau had ordered her to research vitamins and get Sloan to take them. Her guilt increased, and she worked endless hours, fighting for her career at Standards Elite.

The morning wind whipped Melanie's umbrella from her and pasted her raincoat against her body. Rivulets of rain streamed down her hair and face as she struggled to keep her heavy briefcase from being torn from her hands.

Strained and tired, she'd dressed quickly, grabbing a comfortable bra that did not minimize, and chose cotton panties, which did not "firm and mold." Comfortable that her navy blue business suit shielded her femininity, Melanie entered Standards' revolving door just before Sloan.

"Hey, Mel," he said, catching up to her in front of the elevator and stripping his raincoat off. "Are you taking Danielle to the mall tonight?"

"Planning to, Raventhrall," she said, sniffing and wiping rain from her cheek. "There's a sale on white dress gloves for girls. Danielle doesn't have any, nor a proper purse. Hold my briefcase while I take off my raincoat. The rain blew down my collar." She entered the elevator with him and shivered with the chill that had penetrated her clothing.

"Mel?" Sloan said quietly, too quietly beside her as she pushed back a curl from her cheek. He reached out to touch the ringlets coiling on her forehead. "What happened to your hair?"

"It's wet. My umbrella got caught in the bus door, then the wind sailed it toward Alaska," she muttered, fighting to keep her balance as a beefy man pushed her against Sloan.

His hands tightened instantly on her upper arms, steadying her. His body tensed against hers. Sloan's hands pressed her closer.

Her un-minimized breasts slowly eased against his chest.

As in slow motion, Sloan's chin lowered to rest on her wet hair, and Melanie's heart stopped. He allowed her to push inches away, staring down at her face and tracing every feature intently.

He blinked once, looked at her soaked curls and blinked again. He stared at her eyes and asked in a slow, husky whisper, "Where are your glasses?"

"Rain, Raventhrall," she managed, trying to move away. "It streaks them.... Here, let me put them on."

There in the crowded elevator, Sloan's free hand slid to find her breast and curl possessively around it, cupping the soft weight beneath her business jacket.

"Sloan," she whispered unevenly as his expression darkened.

"Sloan," she repeated, pleading as pure rage changed his brown eyes into black.

"You," he said in a quiet, distinct roar between his teeth, the muscle sliding over his jaw. "You."

Five

Inside the paper-and-supplies storage closet where Sloan had shuttled her, Melanie simmered with anger. She jerked her jacket down from where it had risen, high on her unminimized bosom. "Don't ever put a waist lock on me and carry me into a room again, Raventhrall," she said when she could catch her breath. Tucked against Sloan as he moved down the Elite hallway, her feet two inches off the floor, was like being carried by a tornado.

"I don't believe you're in any position to order me to do anything, Inganforde." A muscle slid across his jaw, working rhythmically as he ground his teeth. Dark red crept high on his cheek as he loomed over her, breathing hard.

He opened his tie and collar with the jerk of one finger, his eyes black and gleaming behind thick lashes. There, glaring down at her in the light of a bald, swaying light bulb, Sloan breathed heavily. There was a primitive flare to his nostrils that she had never seen. His anger swirled around her, backing her against the shelves of paper.

He reached out to lock the door, then tossed his brief
case and their coats into the bin marked Recycled Paper
Running both hands through his damp hair until it stood ou
in peaks, Sloan blinked twice, as though trying to place an
other image over hers.

She cleared her throat, fearing his next move. "Ah..
Sloan...are you feeling—"

"Take them off...everything. Strip," he ordered firmly
breathing hard.

"You've had a setback...maybe walking in the rain...
Maybe you should go home, Sloan...." Melanie inched to
ward the door. Sloan narrowed his eyes and with one hand
rolled the paper-recycling bin in front of the door.

Clutching her briefcase, Melanie shivered. In her life
time, she'd never seen a truly enraged male, nor fallen pre
to one. When Sloan advanced one step and ordered again
"Strip," a distinct shiver of fear began at the base of her
spine and worked upward.

"I refuse," she said as he bent to slip off her two-inch
pumps and examine the lifts she wore inside. He slipped th
lifts into his jacket pocket and stared appraisingly at the area
of her chest.

Sloan's toothy, cold smile gleamed above her, reminding
her of a wolf who has found his prey. A hungry wolf, she
corrected, one that shook off his tethers as he would dis
card clinging feathers.

Swallowing again, Melanie pulled up her sleeve and
glanced at her watch. "We'll be late. Devereau wants tha
report on his desk—"

"Damn Devereau," he said tightly, taking the briefcase
away from her and tossing it into the bin.

In an effort at bravado, Melanie stated firmly, "Sloan
you're being—"

"Shy, sweetheart?" he asked too softly, reaching to slide
her jacket from her easily. "Here, let me help you." He
reached to loosen her blouse, pulling it from her skirt. Slid

ing his hands beneath the material, he spanned her small waist, his thumbs caressing her slip and the lower softness of her breasts. "You're a small woman, aren't you, M. S. Inganforde? Small and blond and shapely...."

With that, one large hand closed possessively over her breast with unerring accuracy. She gasped, placing her hands on his chest, and Sloan's taut face darkened as he quickly stripped his jacket away.

Tugging her against him, Sloan fitted her slowly, inch by inch down his hard body. His hands opened on her back, sweeping down slowly to her buttocks and cupping them gently, tracing the size and shape lightly. His chin rested on the top of her head, and he pulled her so close that she was forced to rest against him. "Bratwurst," he muttered above her.

"This won't get you anything, Raventhrall," she managed huskily, refusing to do bodily combat with a newly recovered invalid.

"The hell it won't." Sloan inhaled sharply, his hands slowly unfastening her bra before moving on. Breathing lightly, he found her left breast, slid under the blouse and lace bra to cup her gently. He groaned as though disbelieving his touch, heat racing through him.

Trying to wedge inches from him, Melanie found her hips intimately lifted to his. His hand ran beneath her skirt and upward, gliding over the lacy garter belt supporting her stockings and tracing the tiny red rose low on her stomach. Melanie closed her eyes and wished desperately that the clock were turned back to allow her to stuff herself into the specially tailored underwear and panty hose. Tearing her last pair of panty hose left her with the thigh-high pair tucked back into a corner of her lingerie drawer.

Shuddering against her, Sloan whispered, "God, you're soft, Melanie. All woman and curves. You smell like flowers and make a man want to—"

"Sloan! You aren't feeling well. You really aren't!" she managed, leaning back as he bent over her.

"The hell I'm not." Then he kissed her hungrily, as though time could wait until he'd had his fill of loving her.

There in the tight enclosure, wrapped in Sloan's strong embrace, Melanie's body heated, her heart racing as he kissed her strawberry birthmark. "You've had me tied up in knots," he murmured roughly against the pulse in her throat, nibbling on her earlobe. "No woman tastes like you...will ever taste like you," he corrected. "You've ruined me for life."

He lifted her high then, placing his warm face against her breasts and nuzzling her as though he had found everything he'd ever wanted...intending to savor her for a lifetime.

When his lips found her breast, Melanie tried to breathe...tried to think sensibly. Then she yielded to the moment, gently pressing his head against her, stroking the back of his taut neck as he sighed deeply. "Hold me, Mel. Just hold me," he murmured, pressing a trail of desperate, nibbling little kisses to her other breast.

She began to tighten before his teeth worried her breast...before his warm hand eased low to find her intimately. "Sloan...." she whispered achingly as the hungry fever began to rise, enveloping her.

Sloan. Her life-mate. Her blood and heart, her other half. Melanie threw caution away, flying into the passion he offered, meeting his kisses with the wild abandon driving her.

Images flew at her, splintered and reformed as Sloan made love to her. Diamonds and firelight, Sloan's tanned chest, warmed steel against her lips. The hair covering his chest served to sensitize her hands until she wanted to explore the hard ridges and muscles of his body....

She wanted to touch, to please him—her palms skimmed down his rigid back, tracing the layers of muscle to his waist and firm hips.

Then, irrevocably, her hands slid to his buttocks, lightly testing the taut shape. She lay fully against him, comforted by the vast strength that supported them both, shielded from harm as her love touched her with the greatest care.

Sometime—another century later—Sloan cradled her against him, kissing the perspiration from her forehead. She sagged against him, feeling wonderfully warm and protected. His lips moved in a smile as he stroked her back, holding her carefully, tenderly against him, despite the bold evidence of his passion.

"You were made for me, Inganforde," he whispered, nuzzling her lids, her nose and licking her swollen, tender lips. "It's just a matter of time. You haven't a chance to escape now."

Resting against him, against taut thighs indicating his need, Melanie breathed hard, aware distantly that her breasts lay against his flat stomach, intimately nestled in the hair that sensitized her with every breath.

Struggling for balance and reality, she slowly eased her cheek upward on Sloan's bare shoulder to look at him. His necktie and one button of his shirt remained intact.

Staring at the second button dangling by a thread from his shirt, she stared helplessly into his very pleased expression.

"This moment in time bodes well for our physical love, sweetheart," he whispered in a deep, rumbling purr. "We'll work on our relationship as we go."

Her fingertips quivered, still clenching his broad shoulder, and Melanie forced them to still. She cleared her throat, aware that her legs would not leave Raventhrall's heavy thighs, no matter how much she willed her muscles and bones to move. "What are we going to do, Sloan?" she asked, at a loss to place reality and Sloan-the-infinitely-tender lover in the same era.

"Wade through the bad, my love," he answered cheerfully, patting her bottom lovingly.

Melanie blinked once, trying to dismiss the light pat. The second pat lingered, and she stated carefully, "No one *ever* pats my bottom, Sloan. No one," she said more firmly, drawing away from him.

"Always a first time, darling," he returned easily, his gaze dropping to her unbuttoned blouse and the taut tips of her breasts thrusting against her clothing. There was a distinct edge of anger to his voice, though it was temporarily held at bay. "Your bottom was made for patting, M.S."

Jerking down her blouse with shaking fingers, Melanie stepped back, anger and frustration flaming through her. "Back off, you fiend. I won't be fondled and—"

He smiled then, the wolf's preying smile. "And loved?" he finished. "Well loved, from the looks of it. From the startled look on that wonderful, expressive face, I'd say it was the first time you've felt the earth move in a while. I felt a little quake myself."

Melanie ran her hand across her forehead, wondering if she had truly stepped into another world. Sloan drew her against him, tucked his chin on top of her curls and reached to fasten her bra. "Don't worry, Mel. Things will work out...."

Standing stiffly against him, Melanie refused to be seduced by his warmth, his enticing, woodsy, all-male scent. "No. This can't be, Raventhrall. I refuse to be—"

He held her away and began buttoning her blouse as if he'd performed the task for years. "I'll take care of everything. I've been waiting for—"

"Don't hand me that, Raventhrall," she returned flatly, feeling more like herself as she stepped into her pumps. "You've *never* waited for women. I refuse to be another notch on your belt. I am not your usual type—nothing about me is amazonish."

His expression hardened, a finger reached out to snare a curl as he studied the lights playing in it. "Don't think for a moment that I'm happy to discover your real identity, Inganforde. Because I'm not. You're underhanded, deceiving . . . and the mother of my children on that farm in Iowa. Somewhere in there, I feel rather used and abused. You listened to all my thoughts. . . . God, when I think that M. S. Inganforde is my lover, my nymph—my blood goes cold."

Melanie clenched her fists, then she swatted at his hands as he effectively tucked in her blouse. "Stop wriggling," he ordered darkly. "I have a baby sister whose blouse needed tucking in every time she moved. I'm an expert on taking care of females—that's why they gifted me with Danielle. She just proved a little too much this visit."

"I'll bet you're an expert on females," Melanie muttered, shivering beneath the big hands that smoothed her clothing efficiently.

He slid a finger inside her waistband and jerked, just hard enough to startle her. "Don't push me, Inganforde. I'm a very angry man."

"You think I'm not angry? You've just acted very unprofessional in our place of business—" she began, then stopped as Sloan's dark gaze clung to her mouth . . . as if he wanted to kiss her until doomsday.

"They thought you were walking beside me, sweetheart. No one noticed that your feet didn't touch the ground." Sloan buttoned her top button and ran a proprietary hand down her soft bosom, dismissing her swatting hands. He sighed reluctantly and tugged the curls on top of her head. "You realize that we'll have to work on this courting thing gradually to salve your reputation."

"Courting?" Melanie froze, staring up into Sloan's tender expression.

"Courting, darling," he said firmly, bending to nibble at her lips. "The thing men and women do before they get married. I'm totally confident that we'll be able to work out your little deception to our mutual satisfaction." His smile grew, his eyes gleaming sexily. "I'll wear my coat into the office and you follow."

Crouching near her legs, Sloan recovered his shirt buttons from the floor. Rising slowly, he trailed his palm along her legs, snapping her garter belt before she could swat his hand away. "There." Sloan slid the buttons into her palm, folded it over them and kissed her fist. "You may sew my buttons on my shirt, Mel. Double reinforce them, will you? You're a strong little thing when you—" He smiled again and bent to kiss her lips lightly. "When you want."

"Raventhrall, I will not play maid to you because you've discovered that I dress for the business world. Other women go through the same kinds of things to carve a niche out of a male-dominated occupation—"

He lifted an eyebrow. "Not *my* woman, sweetheart. Not with me. From now on, there won't be any secrets between us. The first thing I'll want to know is why you married and divorced. Since my biological clock is ticking double time now, I'll want to know a little about how you feel about children... but not just yet," he added firmly. "If the way you handle Danielle is anything to go by, you believe in control. Sprinkle attention and cuddling into your methods, add old-fashioned cookie-making and values, and you'll be a perfect mother—"

Shaking with temper, Melanie exploded as Sloan rummaged for his raincoat and slipped into it. She stomped her pumps against the tile floor, clenching her fist. "You egotist. You absolute maniac. What makes you think for a minute that I'll discuss my marriage or children with you?"

He buttoned the coat calmly, then slid her arms into her jacket as though he was dressing a child. He adjusted her business pin carefully, then traced his fingertip across her trembling lips. "You're having a tantrum, Inganforde. A passionate woman occasionally rants at her beloved. That's why I'm here. To take the good with the bad. To cuddle and warm you on cold winter nights...."

She stared at him, gaging the predatory male gleam in his eyes. "You are unbelievable. You really were affected by that flu. You've reverted to the Tarzan and Jane roles, you man, me woman, chest-beating, chauvinistic—"

Scanning her from head to toe and nodding as though he was satisfied, Sloan said, "Make no mistake about it, Inganforde. *I am affected by you, darlin'. You are the future mother of my children on that Iowa farm....*"

"Ohhh!"

She repeated the frustrated sound when he patted her bottom as she preceded him out the door.

At noon, Devereau popped his head into Melanie's office and peered over the huge bouquet of dark, rich roses—minus thorns. "Boyfriend? Secrets, M.S.?" When she stared at him blankly, he continued in a lower voice. "M.S., you look shell-shocked. Maybe you're getting Raventhrall's flu. Hope not. Have you noticed how our star player looks this morning? As if he's on the scent of new profit. Has that bright-eyed, bushy-tailed look, that certain hunter's look, like he's just 'round the bend of something he wants very much.... I love it when Raventhrall acts like a bird dog on point, like one scenting a covey of quail. Oh, by the by, don't forget we're all going to Mr. Bitty's Saturday night. He's really pleased with Standards' work and wants to introduce us to his potential fiancée."

Melanie pictured quail huddled before a huge, muscular hunting dog. "One...." she said dully before realizing she had spoken.

"Eh?"

"Raventhrall wants just one quail, Mr. Devereau," she answered softly with a sigh.

"Must be choice. Nice round, firm profits. Something juicy and well worth the effort drove him out of the doldrums. He can pick the hot ones.... Feels them out and then jumps on 'em before they can slip away.... I'll wait for him to tell me about it...when he's ready. Help Raventhrall out more, when you can, M.S."

During the next half hour, Sloan passed her office several times, his dark hungry gaze pinning her. At twelve-thirty, he entered her office and said, "We're having lunch. I've reserved an intimate little table at Gino's. You're looking pale. You'll feel better after a glass of wine."

The full impact of Sloan arriving to claim her riveted Melanie to her chair. "No. I'm quite happy with my brown-bag fare, thank you."

Sloan leveled his eyebrows down at her, walked around the desk, placed his hands on her waist and lifted her to her feet. "I am a very angry, frustrated man, Inganforde. I recommend that for now you pacify me in these small ways. I haven't quite decided how to handle you just yet. There is the matter of Itty's ownership papers. A man doesn't like to be pushed around by his lover, you know."

"Itty's mine," she returned uneasily, watching him closely.

"True. You have his ownership papers." Sloan ran his fingertip across Melanie's sensitive lips, tension racing between them like a taut electric wire. He circled her throat with his fingers, his thumb resting on the hollow of her throat, smoothing it. "Your skin is like silk, M.S. Warm, soft silk. You are truly the sexiest, most feminine woman I have ever met," he murmured in a tone that doubled her heartbeat. "This should be interesting."

"I'm not a package to be unwrapped for your express...um...undesirable intentions, Sloan," she managed when she could talk.

He lifted her hand and kissed the back, nibbling on her knuckles. "M.S., you are a bonbon that I can't wait to unwrap."

Throughout the romantic lunch, Sloan treated her in a courtly manner, seating her carefully and seeing to her needs. Though his conversation was light, there was a tremor running between them that set her nerves on edge.

His stare traced her face as though remembering. . . . She didn't trust him, not for a moment.

Sloan Raventhrall was an angry man. She couldn't trust him.

Realizing that he wasn't above making a scene, she allowed him to hold her hand beneath the table. Despite everything, Sloan's hand was dependable, a lifeline in turbulent times.

"Don't forget, you're taking Danielle on the white-glove hunt tonight," he reminded her at the end of the day. Then he bent to discreetly kiss her cheek. Against her ear, he whispered, "I haven't quite decided what to do with you, my love. Tread lightly until I do."

"You can't have Itty back," she returned, jerking away.

Sloan smiled benignly. "It's you I want, darlin'. Just little old you."

When she arrived at his apartment, Sloan's appraising gaze slid down her sweater-and-slacks set. Then he drew her into his arms and kissed her tenderly. "Have fun," he said, patting her bottom away from Danielle's curious gaze.

An hour later, Sloan stood in front of Melanie's apartment. After checking the empty hallway, he slid his new key into her lock. Working with the college narcotics squad when he was a student was perfect training for solving Inganforde's mysteries. Getting the wax impression from a key on her ring wasn't difficult, a matter of slipping into her office when she was conferring with Devereau.

M. S. Inganforde's identity had been kept from him long enough, and Sloan wanted to know everything about her. He justified his gambit into her privacy as a repayment. He fully intended to take out the entire measure of his frustration on Melanie's delectable hide—he intended to love her until she longed for him, too. . . but not until he'd unraveled her secrets.

He smiled tightly as the door opened. A master of disguise, Melanie had hidden her charms well. Within moments he would discover her essence, and then he could make plans to capture his nymph. He deserved the bit of revenge for her deception. After tonight, he intended to play a fair game with her . . . one that he intended to win.

He leaned against the doorway of the foyer, inhaling the light flowery scent of a nymph's hiding place. Soft lighting spread over the room like muted sunshine. Creams, light mauves and blended pale greens gave an impression of soft roominess. Tropical plants spread everywhere. Sheer panels kept the harsh Kansas City lights at bay. Behind the light mauve overstuffed couch, a fresh bouquet of daisies and ferns towered over an array of various gold picture frames. Sloan noted the starched doily under the frames.

A chubby, curly-haired blond girl of five or so hugged the cat dangling over her arm. A taller boy, sturdy and bored, stood with her, and two matching proud parents stood behind the children. Melanie's high school graduation picture, complete with family, years older now, sat near a picture of the boy, dressed in a football uniform. Two small blond children were propped in the arms of a smiling man and woman. . . . The older couple, posed in a formal setting and framed elegantly, stood near them. The woman, Melanie and another man, captured under a spreading shade tree, caught Sloan's attention. The woman and Melanie were alike: petite, delicate, voluptuous blondes.

Sloan noted with satisfaction that there were no pictures of a man holding Melanie against him possessively.

He studied the books lining one wall. Titles like *Professional Dress, Women in Business, Petites Go for It, Petites—Big in Business* and *The Small Woman Competes with Giants* dominated her shelves. Gilt-bound copies of Robert Burns's poetry and other romance books spread over one shelf.

A small turtle watched Sloan from his terrarium as the man picked up Melanie's embroidery hoop to study the intricate pale flowers on the pillowcase. A sewing machine occupied a corner of the room, a half-finished concoction of pink ruffles and lace lying beneath its needle.

Shamefully neat, the pale yellow kitchen reminded Sloan of a country home, wooden utensils standing in a pottery bowl, a brass tea kettle with delicate spout sitting on a stove designed for cooking. He bent to study a variety of handwritten recipes that Melanie was neatly logging into a write-your-own cookbook. A row of African violets in various blues and fuchsias rested on a shelf near a window. Filled with lentils, pasta, and beans, antique blue jars were lined up next to a bowl of fresh fruit. Opening the refrigerator, Sloan stared at the contents, neatly arranged on the shelves. He reached in to take a juicy strawberry, savored it while he thought of things he intended to do to Melanie's birthmark. Then, smiling grimly, he moved down the hallway to the bedroom.

A huge four-poster bed with a hand-sewn quilt dominated the room. Picking up a ruffled granny gown lying across a crocheted afghan, Sloan smoothed the rosebud pattern. Delicately shaped feminine bottles and jars, neatly arranged on a mirror, occupied a small wooden vanity. Sloan replaced the gown carefully, his hand lingering over it. He moved to study the brush on the vanity table, and for an instant he thought of brushing his lover's hair as they rested on the four-poster. A familiar womanly scent startled him when he opened the door to the bathroom.

Melanie liked to soak in bubble baths. Sloan lifted the stopper on the bath salts, memorizing the heady fragrance. He glanced at the scented candles and noted the romantic tape in the small tape cassette player before he closed the door quietly.

M. S. Inganforde was still hiding from him, and Sloan carefully opened the top drawer of her well-polished dresser.

Delicate, lacy lingerie in delicate beiges and virginal whites were neatly folded and stacked over his contract with Itty. He opened a larger drawer and discovered the method she had used to resemble a bratwurst sausage.

Sloan tested the sturdy material, placing his two hands inside the girdle and forcing them apart. He studied the construction and heavy material of the bra, trying to control his raging anger and the need to rip it to shreds. He opted to let M. S. Inganforde perform the task willingly.

After checking to see that everything was just as he had found it, Sloan left the apartment.

He would truly enjoy snaring Melanie S. Inganforde and treating her to the lifetime of love that she richly deserved.

"Things are definitely out of hand," Melanie muttered, painting a final coat of Posie Pink on her toenails. Sloan had to be stopped. She thought better with neatly pedicured toenails lined up beneath her, and Sloan Raventhrall, on the hunt, needed to be foiled.

"Now that he's up to his old ball game, maybe he'll switch to amazons," she stated, plucking a list of potential candidates from the quilt beside her. "An amazon a day will keep the wolf away," she sing-songed, snuggling down in her grandmother's best hand-sewn quilt. She studied the list and sighed. No woman worth her perfume and lace teddy could resist Sloan Raventhrall in a romantic mood.

She placed the list aside, snapped off her bedside light and stared at the moon.

Sloan's kisses tasted of tenderness and romance, with just the right touch of rough hunger to remind her that he was a man who wanted her desperately. Holding his needs at bay was incredibly sweet and thoughtful of him. Adjusting to thoughts of Sloan sharing her bed—and her life—caused her to shiver.

Predatory, courtly, possessive and gentle all described Sloan's behavior.

Melanie frowned in the dark. She really did not like that stealthy, fond little pat on the bottom when he was near her. She reached to twirl a fat curl around her fingers and thought of the way Sloan's eyes darkened as his hands slid through her hair. Then there was the hot, draining, sweet-lover kiss that started as a nibble on her lower lip and worked itself into a full-blown possessive hunger.

She turned onto her stomach, drawing a large, soft pillow against her for comfort. Sloan in a romantic mood was just too much, she thought drowsily, snuggling against the pillow. Since it was Friday night, she would have the weekend to recover and plan her anti-Sloan campaign.

The telephone rang, and Melanie answered it sleepily. Sloan's deep tones poured intimately over the lines. "I miss you, sweetheart, and I love you. Whatever happens, remember that. I'll pick you up at five o'clock tomorrow evening for Itty's party. El Lobo is baby-sitting. He and Danielle are using your oatmeal-and-raisin cookie recipe—"

"I'm not going with you. I have my own transportation, thank you," she returned primly.

"You drive that Beetle like a mad hornet, Inganforde," he returned, unscathed by her rejection. "This is your coming-out party and you'll ride with me."

"Stop dishing out orders, Raventhrall. You drive a truck. A big, black, tall beast.... I'd need a ladder to get down. Once we took it to a trade show and you laughed at me, remember?"

"I won't laugh tomorrow night," he promised after what she decided was a muffled chuckle. She hated that deep, purring, all-male sound.

"Because I'm not—repeat, *not*—going with you. Gossip would run through Standards like the flu."

He gnawed on that for a full second before returning smoothly, "Itty wouldn't like knowing that you're a black-mailer, sweetheart."

"You're demented," she whispered after a gasp.

"True."

"You're not going to have your way all the time, Raven-thrall," she stated firmly, replacing the receiver.

That night, she dreamed of Raventhrall's big black truck charging through the mists, headlights slicing over the wet Kansas City streets. Like a Ninja warrior, dressed in sheer black, Sloan scaled her apartment building and levered himself into her room to bring her a lush bouquet of thorn-less roses.

Scattering the fragrant petals across her bed, Sloan joined her there, the gold wedding band on his dark hand match-ing hers. He moved over her with a certainty born of a wel-coming lover— Melanie awoke suddenly to the sound of her sighs and the desperate ache within her.

Shivering in reaction, she closed her eyes. "Oh, please . . . please . . . not Sloan Raventhrall," she whispered desperately. She tested her forehead with her palm. "Maybe I'm coming down with the flu. Oh, I really hope I am."

Six

Melanie watched Sloan's capable, large hands easily control his black monster as they charged across Kansas City's slick streets to Itty's palacelike home.

She frowned slightly, noting the unrelenting grasp of his dark fingers on the black leather steering wheel. She'd planned to arrive at Itty's alone and leave in the same manner. Finding Sloan on her doorstep an hour early, his hand offering a huge bouquet of daisies to her, blocked off her various methods of escaping his grasp.

She fidgeted in her seat, adjusting the washable jade-green silk shirtdress primly around her knees. If only the daisies hadn't seduced her instantly.... If only she hadn't exclaimed with delight, "Oh, Sloan...."

Crossing her arms protectively over her chest, Melanie stared through the slightly foggy windows. The city's neon lights glimmered on the rain-slick streets. It wasn't fair of Sloan to use daisies as bait, especially the huge Cascade variety with fern greenery. She glowered savagely at a woman with a benign, grandmotherly smile who stood at a street crossing. The pleasure darkening Sloan's eyes as they traveled down her modestly cut, long-sleeved dress was possessive and totally sensual, making her feel like an exotic, delicious bonbon. His expression resembled that of a sheik anticipating his cherished bride on their wedding night.

As they stopped at a red light, Melanie continued to wallow in her dark mood. She slashed a frown at a six-year-old boy who held his mother's hand as they crossed the street.

Raventhrall had to be stopped, and soon.

Sliding a stealthy look at the accused, Melanie snuggled deeper in the protective recesses of her raincoat and the shadows. He'd filled her apartment, stepping into it with that damned huge, beguiling bouquet of daisies. Dressed in a casual black jacket, slacks and sweater, Sloan had a suave, living-on-the-edge look. Like Humphrey Bogart in a taller, leaner version. Something inside her had definitely quivered when he entered her apartment. Sloan looked delicious and slightly... dangerous.

He'd stared down at her with an unconcealed fascination, taking in the hair that resisted her attempts to control it, the modest lines of her shirtwaist dress. For just a nanosecond, Sloan's expression was sheer pleasure.

She'd reacted shamelessly, instantly and unexplainably pleased that she'd spent hours working with the delicate fabric and indulging in her favorite bath salts. Her Posie Pink-tinted toenails seemed to warm within her high-heeled shoes.

When he'd handed her the bouquet, that darned bit of uncertainty flickered beneath his long, silky lashes. There was just something enchanting about Sloan, the wary male surrounded by ruffly, unfamiliar homeyness. He had sniffed appreciatively, testing the freshly baked apple pie aroma, and gazed longingly toward the pie cooling in her kitchen.

She adjusted her glasses primly. Somehow that flash of uncertainty reached out and snagged a vulnerable cell in her heart. She'd wanted to curl against him, hold him tightly and reassure him that she was deeply pleased.

Closing her eyes, Melanie listened to the windshield wipers slapping away and tried to forget the way Sloan had picked her up and gently deposited her in the black monster's front seat. He touched her as if concentrating deeply on how to touch her, as though she were a fragile petal of one of those wonderful daisies. Yet there was a savageness underlying his touch, as if he'd draw and quarter anyone who tried to wrest her away from him.

Melanie looked out at the streets, trying to avoid the thought that no man had ever treated her as courtly as Sloan Raventhrall, amazon specialist, was treating her now. He could ambush her when she least expected, leaving her amid emotions she didn't understand. She firmed her lips. Quivering and throbbing didn't suit her M. S. Inganforde image.

"Yo, Melanie," Sloan interrupted, his hand lowering from the back of the seat to caress her shoulder. "What's causing the gloom?"

Since she saw no reason to conceal her current problem with Sloan, she turned to him and answered, "I hate frogs and I hate princes. If you're expecting any...thank-you's later tonight, forget it."

He laughed outright, an indulgent, caressing sound that raised the hairs on the back of her neck. "I love it when you talk dirty."

"Just getting the terms of our relationship—for the evening—out in the open, Raventhrall. Other than finishing my stint as Danielle's pseudo-aunt, and passing each other in the office, we have no relationship. None."

Curiosity flickered in his dark eyes as they traced her face in the shadows. "Our relationship...just what is it?"

"Business," she answered primly and plucked at the burnished buckle on her silk purse. The sprawling lights of Itty's southern-style mansion appeared, and Sloan turned into the open gates of the driveway. "And Danielle, of course."

"Really?" he asked in a sensual drawl, twirling one dark finger through a fat curl and testing it gently with his thumb. "You fidget when you're fibbing, Inganforde. And when you're nervous. I don't suppose you'd come over here and let me cuddle you while you're in this snit, would you?"

Melanie stared at him frostily. "I am not Danielle."

"Honey, you're bristling," Sloan stated benignly as he guided the beast into a tiny parking spot on Itty's elegant driveway. He turned off the engine and looked at her, lifting her glasses off her nose and tucking them in his pocket. "You don't need these. . . . They're glass, part of your hide-the-beauty disguise." His finger brushed her cheek. "I suppose it isn't easy in our business—a petite, blue-eyed blonde would have a difficult time. . . ." he mused, as though to himself.

Then he smiled, that beguiling, charming smile that attracted women like bees to honey. "You're a beautiful woman when you're confused and furious, Mel. You look like you'd ignite if I touched you."

"I took a karate class last February," she answered loftily. "Don't mess with me. I could break your wrist, just like that," she added, snapping her fingers.

"Uh-huh." Sloan eased from his seat, and before she could move, he'd plucked her into his arms, carrying her through the rain to Itty's sprawling porch.

"Put me down," she whispered furiously when she finally managed to speak. "I'll destroy you. . . . I'll . . ."

Sloan held her for a moment, his arms tightening. His kiss tasted her parted lips, cherished her sweetly. When Melanie could at last open her eyes, she lay curled against him, her arms holding his neck tightly. Sloan rubbed her nose with his and whispered shakily, "I'm as frightened as you are, sweetheart. We'll be fine."

Melanie blinked, trying to understand something beyond the warmth of Sloan's body as he placed her carefully on her feet and smoothed her raincoat.

When Itty opened the door, reaching out his beefy hand to draw her into the mansion, Melanie found herself shuttled along between the two tall men. A butler, dressed in formal black and wearing an impassive expression, took her coat while she tried to deal with Sloan's gentle kiss. While he ambled along at her side, she sensed that with the first move she made away from him, he would reclaim her without explanation to anyone. She also sensed Sloan's protective attitude and the easy way he dismissed their joint appearance. "Sharing rides...saving gas..."

Itty chugged along ahead of them, growling introductions and breaking a wide swath to his gay-nineties-style poolroom, which was crowded with an odd assortment of people, ranging from business types to those of questionable professions. Without his usual cigar smoke, Itty's tough ex-con image slipped a little. The excitement in his gravelly voice and the luminous glow settling over his craggy features created an endearing, grandfatherly image. Over Melanie's head, he ordered Sloan, "My bride-to-be doesn't like smoke and boozers. You spot anyone lighting up and you snuff it out, got it? Don't waste time sobering anyone up, just call that fancy butler of mine. He knows what to do. A class act with no noise."

He leaned closer to Sloan, who had moved so close to Melanie that his hand brushed her bottom in a slow, concealed caress. Itty continued, speaking confidentially over the tones of Ella Fitzgerald and the crowd's loud rumble, "My baby has been married twice...husbands died...thinks she's bad luck and doesn't want to get hitched again. She's squeaky-clean, the wholesome type...makes me feel ten feet tall, like a kid, you know. Plays five-card draw like a pro...cooks great, knows how to jitterbug. A real classy beauty, but tough, you know? The kind of woman who won't run when things get tough. I want to be a lifer with no parole. Tonight, she's my hostess," he added proudly.

Itty leaned down to Melanie and showed his teeth. "This is the scam, see? You guys set me up as Mr. Perfect Husband. I haven't met her kids yet, but her girl lives somewhere here in the city.... I always wanted kids—maybe a boy like old Raventhrall here. Maybe a sweet little babe like you, Peaches."

Suddenly Itty frowned, studying Melanie, from curling blond hair down her curvy, voluptuous body to her small feet. "Well, I'll be a St. Louie judge...."

"Don't get any ideas, Itty. She's mine." Sloan moved closer, his jaw locked as his eyes narrowed. Melanie looked up, surprised by the image of a primitive male bristling when his territory was invaded.

Itty straightened, stared at Sloan and blinked as though remembering his current time zone. He glanced down at Melanie warily. "This should be interesting," he said quietly before turning and blazing a trail toward the pool table.

"Sloan. Back off," Melanie hissed, easing away from his hand that had clamped to her waist as he drew her into the protection of his body. "I can handle myself."

"Sure," he muttered, watching Itty cut another swath toward them, dragging a small blond woman in his wake. The woman was vaguely familiar to Melanie. Bodies and Itty's bulk alternately blocked and revealed glimpses of a woman dressed in a black, tasteful dress and wearing pearls.

Sloan's arm dragged Melanie closer, as though he were a pirate ready to carry his captive princess aboard his ship while swinging his deadly cutlass....

Itty took a deep breath, stared at Melanie intently and tugged on the small, feminine hand within his grasp. Stepping from behind Itty's bulk, Delilah Burns met her daughter's matching cerulean blue eyes and said breathlessly, "Oh, my...*oh, my!*"

"Mother?"

"Melanie?"

"Mother?" Sloan and Itty repeated, looking from mother to daughter and back again.

"Delilah Burns, your bride-to-be, Itty, is my mother. She remarried when I was a year old.... Burns is my stepfather's name and my half brother's."

Delilah's eyes widened, panic spreading across her delicate features. "Melanie Inganforde, please don't get angry. You know how you can be.... I was going to call...."

Melanie stared up at Itty, whose expression resembled a pleading tomcat out in the rain and fearing that his last hope for food would be tossed into the garbage. Her mother's eyes began to dampen suspiciously. Melanie shook free of Sloan's protective body and tapped her foot. She didn't attempt to keep the anger from her voice. "Mother, please explain...now. Just how long have you been seeing Mr. Bitty? And why did you...hide behind my back? *Just what are you doing here? In his home? Acting as Itty's hostess?*"

"Damn," Sloan muttered quietly to Itty.

"The jig is up," Itty added forlornly.

"You're upset, Melanie," Delilah said quietly, straightening her shoulders. "I knew you would be. I was going to break the news to you this trip."

Melanie waved her hand airily. "Break the news to me? Oh, right. Like you and Mr. Bitty are an item, and *I don't know my own mother is involved with a prospective husband?*"

Delilah crossed her arms across her ample breasts and tapped her small, high-heeled shoe. "Please don't raise your voice, Melanie. You'll distress Itty. Perhaps we could discuss my relationship with Itty over a nice glass of wine...or a game of poker. Take your pick."

"Mother! We're not discussing careers here. You haven't dated since Dad passed away."

Delilah patted Itty's beefy forearm. "There, there, sweetie. Calm yourself. You'll learn that Melanie's bark is worse than her bite. She's really quite reasonable."

"She scares me," Itty muttered, looking at Sloan for help. "Do something, Raventhrall. If she hurts me, it's on your head. Standards will lose all my accounts."

"Fight. Clear the room," Sloan calmly ordered the butler who was looming nearby. Itty cursed beneath his breath, fear oozing out of him like sweat while the butler herded the crowd out of the room and firmly closed the massive, carved doors.

Delilah smiled up at Sloan and asked gently, "Have you learned about her temper yet? She was always such a passionate child."

"The name is Sloan Raventhrall... I'm going to marry your daughter. She needs me to control her passions." Sloan reached out to take Delilah's small hand and shake it. "With your approval, of course. We'll want the whole wedding routine... white lace dress..."

"We'll have it here. I'm buying.... Delilah, set it up," Itty offered. "Spare no expense—"

"I am not marrying Raventhrall," Melanie stated, recognizing the plot to throw her off the scent of her mother's trail. She stared at the wickedly huge square-cut diamond weighting her mother's hand. "Mother!" she shrieked in a whisper.

"Beautiful, isn't it?" Delilah asked, raising on tiptoe to kiss Itty's cheek. "Now that you know, dear, are you pleased? Or do you want to pick away at the details like you always do, lining them up in neat little lists and probing for pros and cons?"

While Melanie gasped, Sloan muffled a suspicious chuckle that changed into a groan when she jabbed him in the ribs. "Damn it, Mel. You hurt me."

"Really?" she asked sweetly, then jabbed him again.

"Poker, anyone?" Delilah interrupted. "Melanie has a right to be upset, and a good game always seems to leaven her out. Some of our better mother-daughter discussions took place over a good game. We love each other deeply and this little problem will work itself out."

"This isn't the way to learn that one's mother has become engaged, you know," Melanie stated loftily as she shuffled the cards later. Her hands moved deftly, depositing the cards on the green felt-covered table. Itty and Sloan shared a silent statement as the two women moved into a methodical, expert first hand. The third hand they squared off, sorting out the proper methods of mothers telling daughters about impending marriages, and the men played quietly.

For some odd reason, tonight Melanie welcomed Sloan's presence. There was something reassuring about his warmth and size sitting next to her. Rather like a Saint Bernard rescue dog near a freezing, lost soul. She had the impression she could crumble into his arms and expect to be comforted and stroked while she—

"I've waited for years for the right man to come along, Melanie. I told you as much when I first met Itty in January. Do you need cards, dear?"

Itty hesitantly slipped two cards to the center of the table, and Delilah dealt another two in quick order, her diamond blazing.

"I fold," Sloan murmured, tossing his cards on the table and settling back as the women raised the bid.

"Fold," Itty ventured, glancing warily at Sloan.

"Are you in, Melanie?" Delilah asked as though she were offering cookies and milk.

Melanie studied her cards. "It's the method of the presentation, Mother. You know I don't like surprises. Raise you," she said, adding two blue chips to the growing pile in the center of the table.

"I can't jitterbug alone, dear. Itty is wonderful," Delilah answered. "He's terribly light on his feet. Such a gentleman. Then he's so appealing—muscular, broad shoulders, little ... hips...."

Itty stared at Delilah. "I am more than a piece of beefcake, pumpkin," he muttered uneasily.

She reached to pat his hand. "Of course, you are. You have brains, lambkins. It's just that you're such a hunk... a dreamboat ... and a wonderful, virile man."

"Virile? What the hell does that mean? I've been healthy all my life."

"Royal flush," Melanie muttered, spreading her cards on the table. A neat stack of white chips tumbled, and she glared at it. "It means that my mother would like to strip you naked and—"

"Melanie! Please don't embarrass Itty. He's delicate," Delilah ordered gently.

Itty blushed and Sloan chuckled again.

"Are you marrying my daughter soon?" Delilah asked Sloan as he dealt another hand. "With luck, I could be a grandmother next year."

He hesitated a moment, then flashed a heart-stopping grin at Delilah. "We're still in the courting stage. She hasn't decided she wants me."

"Yuck." Melanie stared at Itty with open curiosity. "Can you really jitterbug?" When he nodded seriously, she said, "Mother has had a difficult time finding a proper partner and she does love to jitterbug.... It may take time to get used to the idea of mother dating ... marrying again. Please understand."

"I love Itty. He's such a dear," Delilah said quietly, holding Melanie's hand. "Thank you."

Melanie cried all the way to her apartment. She allowed Sloan to use her keys to open her door. Then he was taking her coat and stripping his jacket off to cuddle and hold her on his lap.

She sniffed and leaned her head against his shoulder. "I hate crying."

Sloan's arms tightened around her, his hand drawing her knees across his lap. He slipped off her shoes and massaged her toes. "I know," he said, unsnapping her garters and rolling her sheer stockings down her legs.

He held her while they watched the rain streak down her windows, the neon lights spreading rhythmically across the panes. "I'll miss her," Melanie whispered tiredly as she let Sloan deal with the matter of easing them to a prone position on her couch.

"You have me," he offered quietly as he tucked her against his side and drew the afghan over them. His shoes clunked as they hit the floor.

"I can't work with Itty... not since I know that he's probably seducing my poor, innocent mother right now. I saw her slip, it was black lace... she hasn't ever worn black lace.... She should have left with us. I should never have agreed to let her cut the cards to decide if she'd stay with Itty. She always gets high card.... She could have stayed with me... she usually does, you know. We play poker until dawn, feast on German chocolate cake with pecan frosting and watch moldy oldies when it rains."

"I'll watch moldy oldies with you, honey," Sloan offered sleepily, cuddling her closer. "You can work with Itty. You've already proven it. He's recommending you to others."

"He's afraid of me now. He'll go for anything I suggest. The game won't be fun anymore," Melanie reasoned, placing her hand over the reassuring slow *thump-thump* of Sloan's heart. "It won't be the same without her. She was always there in the middle of the night—just a telephone area code or two away—until lately."

"I make a good listener in the middle of the night. It's my best time...." Sloan's large, warm hand caressed her spine soothingly. "By the way, why did you divorce good old Rick?" he asked while she dealt with losing her mother and acquiring Itty into the family.

"He just wasn't a lover...we were really more like friends who got married when everyone else did," she answered automatically, having thought out the situation long ago. "Adenoid problems, snoring, flabby body.... I couldn't see having his children or spending the rest of my life without that special excitement. Worst of all, he didn't like my family recipe for apple pie."

Sloan nuzzled the top of her curls with his chin, inhaling gently as he continued stroking and soothing her. "I love apple pie."

Melanie sniffed again, noting that Sloan's pleasant warmth had seeped into her, making her feel warm and cherished.

"You shouldn't have told my mother that we're getting married, Sloan. You don't know her." Melanie eased across Sloan's body and stood alone in the dark, staring out into the rainy night.

She was angry suddenly. Charged with the need to push Sloan to the very edge, the way he had pushed her. Rick had never pushed back, and tonight she needed that dangerous edge. She resented Sloan's ability to comfort and cozen her when she needed a really good argument. "You may leave now, Raventhrall. Go," she said quietly, elegantly, with classic-movie drama.

She hadn't heard him move, and suddenly he was looming behind her in the night.

She really resented his ability to make her feel small and helpless. "You should be happy that everything turned out so awful."

"Honey, you're tired and overwrought," Sloan murmured warily, reaching out to cup her shoulders. "Take it easy. Maybe a hot cup of water would settle you down."

She pivoted on him. "Don't you dare try to pacify me, you...you blackmailer...you pirate." She slashed a small hand in front of him. "I'm not the least bit amazonish. I don't know why you delight in torturing me, but *you will leave my apartment this moment.*"

Sloan tilted his head and pushed his hand through his hair. "Damn it, Mel. I was just trying to comfort you in your time of need. That's what lovers are for, sweetheart—"

She stomped her foot. *"You are not my lover... my anything, Raventhrall. I like it that way!"*

"Sweetheart, you're being illogical.... Tonight was just a little difficult..." Sloan looked desperate, just the way Melanie wanted him to look, his hair peaking out at angles from his head. Then he added the final, ultimate challenge to an angry woman. "Ah...maybe it's...ah, that time of the—"

"What?"

Sloan cleared his throat and looked away. "Now, sweetheart, there are certain emotions in the female that run amok when—"

"Amok?" Melanie clenched her hands at her sides. "You are definitely not my type, Raventhrall," she stated flatly. "You with your bodacious amazons and bits of notes. Standards's star, indeed. By the way, I've always hated that thin tie with the polka dots on it. It looks like a G-string."

For the first time, Sloan narrowed his eyes, his body tensing as he loomed over her. She had a quick impression of smoke and fire and shattering passion. "Take it easy, honey," he said through his teeth. "You're not being logical...."

Warming up to her delicious fit of raging temper, Melanie threw caution to the winds. Raventhrall was responding quite nicely to her barbs, his hard face dark with anger. She wondered then what it would take to send him totally over the edge—she'd never experienced the sheer excitement of probing the ultimate limits of Sloan's patience, but somehow tonight seemed a perfect time to issue her challenge.

Sloan ran his hand through his hair again and scowled down at her. She faced him with a fearless, taut smile. "Tonight is not turning out the way I had planned, sweetheart," he stated in a slow, dangerous purr. "Maybe we'd better wait for this discussion until you feel better...maybe after we take Danielle to the zoo tomorrow...."

"You will not try to pacify me, Raventhrall," she ordered, a happy little voice inside her urging her on.

Sloan's eyes narrowed. "Are you challenging me, Inganforde?" he asked softly, snaring her against his taut body. He lifted her up in his arms and strode toward the bedroom.

Melanie just caught her breath when Sloan dropped her onto her grandmother's patchwork quilt. His added weight caused the antique four-poster bed to quake. "This won't solve anything, Raventhrall," she stated bravely, aware that she had stepped into a dangerous realm where the swashbuckling Errol Flynn type—rather, Sloan Raventhrall—was fully aroused.

His body rose above her in the shadows, settling with delicate ease on her. When she squirmed, Sloan closed his eyes and inhaled sharply. "Stop. I can't think when you move like that. I'm trying to be a gentleman."

Then he kissed her gently, tenderly, seductively. While the kiss tempted and soothed and caressed, Melanie wanted more. She wanted the full tempest that she sensed Sloan could provide. She wanted all the equatorial thunderbolts, the fire and the satin. She wanted the ultimate, though she sensed Sloan leashed his passion, taking great care not to hurt or shock her.

Testing her passion-arousing powers for the first time in her life, Melanie parted her lips and bit Sloan's bottom lip. He tensed, his arms shaking slightly with the effort of holding his full weight from her.

Melanie bit his ear delicately and Sloan groaned, his hand rising beneath her slip to her thigh. He caressed the soft flesh there, his fingers trembling. His thumb ran across her intimately, testing the damp cotton briefs.

Then he was kissing her the way she wanted, with thunderbolts and hunger, his hands gently stripping her, his lips finding her breast.

Then, rising against her intimately, Sloan cradled her face in his hands and studied her carefully. "Is this what you want, honey?" he asked unevenly, his face taut with desire.

Melanie nuzzled his sweater, inhaling the soap and scent of his body. "No," she murmured against the warm cove of his throat and shoulder. "I want everything."

"Shoot," he said quietly, sucking in air hard as her hands stroked the sweater from him and attempted to unbutton his slacks. Then he was undressed, lifting her to place her on the violet patterned sheets.

She welcomed him, circling his shaking body with soft limbs and softer murmurs.

Poised intimately above her, Sloan ran a possessive hand down her body as though claiming her for his own. "Come here," he ordered softly, watching her intently from beneath his lashes. It was her moment to choose.

She sensed this moment would set the foundations of their relationship, linking them irrevocably, mystically. Sloan waited, the muscles of his back rigid beneath her palms. "There will be no forgetting this happened in the morning, sweetheart," he warned in a deep rasp. "It's your call."

"Raise you," she whispered, echoing a poker term to up the betting.

Sloan smiled softly in the shadows above her and eased into her until she gasped, stretching to accommodate his power. "Tell me you want me," he ordered. "Show me, Melanie...show me how you want me...." he whispered raggedly, with just the right wisp of vulnerability to make her bold.

Lifting her hips, Melanie tugged the back of his neck, urging him closer.

They lay poised and unmoving, reveling in the form and fit of female and male, silk and steel. Then Melanie pressed gently on his hips, urging him deeper, and Sloan closed his eyes for an instant.

He was her lover then, her other half, making her complete.

Seven

———

Sloan tried to breathe, dragging air into his lungs. He lay tangled with Melanie's soft, moist body, amid her flowery scents and their lovemaking...in the center of her four-poster bed. One dainty, high arch rubbed his calf sensuously.

She smoothed his back, kissed his brow and whispered all the soothing things he'd waited to hear for an eternity.

"Sweetheart," she whispered gently into his ear, after nibbling it until he felt like purring. "I won't break."

"You're small," he muttered, trying to gather strength to lift his weight away from crushing her. "I think we should approach this by gradual steps...."

Against her breast, Sloan frowned, trying to place logic in what had just happened—what was happening now. In his sexual expertise, he'd never had the experience of beginning another explosion before he'd recovered from the first event. Melanie's small, tight body had responded beautifully, rocketing off with his into the pink equatorial clouds.

She moved slightly, and Sloan discovered his need rising quickly. He kissed the delicate, full shape of her breast, contemplating his surprise and hunger while gently running his tongue across her hardened nipples. He studied the pebbly shape, dwelling on the mauve-tipped beauty.

He'd intended to make love to her until the ultimate moment. But even now, when he should be easing away, cuddling her and whispering sweet nothings, he needed every silky, hungry, hot, welcoming inch of her. He moved experimentally, testing the snug fit of their bodies.

Melanie's hands locked him in place. "Darling, you haven't hurt me. I'm really quite sturdy. Could we try that again? Though your restraint is admirable, and I...well, you know...I'm afraid I..." The delicate quiverings surrounding Sloan's strength increased.

He blinked, raising to look down on her. She gently eased back a damp, tousled wave, her expression loving and soft.

"Thank you for that kindness, Melanie," he muttered, uneasy with the fact that he had taken her without a candlelight dinner and the courtly manner he had planned. "But I wanted our first time to be something you'd never forget. Things got out of hand...."

"Oh, posh and double posh." Her hands slid down, brushing him. The excitement and hunger in her eyes frightened him slightly. It was at odds with the ruffled pillow shams and the virginal violets splayed across everything. Melanie's soft shoulder gleamed in the scant light, and Sloan covered it against the night chill.

"You're playing with fire, Inganforde," he warned. "I'm trying to be a gentleman." She was perfect, right down to her unpierced earlobes. Small, soft and untouched, the sight of them devastated him. Pale and hidden as Melanie had been, when nibbled properly they stoked the passions of a hungry woman. Drifting pleasantly in the knowledge that she'd wanted him, Sloan turned his calf slightly so that her dainty little arch could rub his ankle. He wondered if he could compose a successful "Ode to Melanie's Earlobes."

Melanie looked up at him from beneath her lashes and moved luxuriously, seductively beneath him. Blond curls fanned out on the pillow, fragrant with a flowery scent as she raised her hips. She met his tentative thrust and licked his lips like a cat supping cream. Sloan found his hand wandering over the silky flesh to cup her soft hips and gently lift her to him.

"I've never had the chance to be a real, honest to goodness wanton, Raventhrall. It's rather fun."

"Melanie," he said helplessly as she drew him deeper.

"Damn," he cursed silently sometime later while she napped, curled against him, her soft legs tangled with his bulky, hairy ones. "This is going all wrong."

Sloan closed his eyes, then studied her brass bedside clock. He calculated the time roughly and groaned, aware that her small hand had slipped low on his stomach. Since he had dropped her on the four-poster less than an hour ago, they had made love twice. "Twice," he muttered, unhappy about his failed night of romance.

"Mmm?" Melanie purred, nuzzling his chest and sliding over on top of him.

Sloan closed his eyes again, savoring the soft drape of her limbs, the delicate butterfly kisses along his throat and jaw. He stroked her flaring hips and lush, soft bottom, aware that Melanie was experimenting, finding just the right position to accept him fully.

"Stop," he yelled in an uneven whisper. "Honey, this isn't good for you...." His eyes opened wide. Suddenly, Sloan realized that he hadn't told her the most important thing. "I love you, Melanie. You've got to believe me.... I apologize—ah...ah..." Sloan forgot everything but the sweet, silky body testing him ultimately.

Sloan awoke just as dawn hovered beyond the closed blinds. He stretched luxuriously, his hand already searching the warm nest of tangled blankets for Inganforde. He wanted to snuggle and cuddle, and to whisper all those sweet endearments that had flown out the window with his good intentions. He wanted to draw her sweet, soft little creamy body into the spoon of his and rock her gently, while they whispered and planned their future. He wanted to wallow in the four-poster bed, savoring each scent, each luxurious moment of elegance, remembering the pleased, feminine sounds that raised his ego.

"Your pie, Raventhrall," Melanie stated in her crisp business voice somewhere above him. "Then we need to talk. Since I am still serving as Danielle's pseudo-aunt, we have to talk about terms," she said firmly, while he hovered between reality and the night's past events.

"You're driving me nuts, Inganforde," he muttered, taking the pie from her hand and placing it on the bedside table. In the next instant, he jerked slightly on Melanie's fragile wrist and she sprawled in a soft heap of lace and ruffles beside him. "What's this thing?" he asked, probing the old-fashioned, long nightgown with interest. Beneath the voluminous folds, Melanie's small body shivered in response to his explorations.

She scrambled out of bed just as he began inching the frothy yards of prim cotton up her thigh. "Sloan, you are a beast." The cold pie plate was thrust on his stomach and Sloan sighed, drawing himself up to rest on the pillows and the polished headboard of the four-poster.

He studied Melanie with interest. Everything was perfectly in place—the maidenly blush, the swollen soft lips, the delicate shadows beneath her slightly dazed blue eyes. Her tousled curls shimmered in the dim light, her bosom alternately lifted and lowered the soft cotton lying across it. He tested a juicy cinnamon wedge of crust and apples and asked, "Yes, my love?"

Her blush deepened. "Now, Raventhrall. You realize we're in a delicate situation...." She glanced warily at him. "I take responsibility for last night. You mustn't blame yourself.... You mustn't feel obliged to treat me in any way different. We've worked together for three years and we can continue to function."

"Function? Is that what we just did?" Sloan finished the pie and placed the empty plate beside the bed. He levered out of bed in one movement and walked toward Melanie, who had backed against a wall. He placed one hand on either side of her head and studied her determined, flushed, uncertain expression. "Have you made your lists this morning, Mel—dear? Placed everything in different columns? Did you weigh the pros and cons?"

She glanced down uneasily. "Ah... Sloan, could we talk about this when you're dressed?"

"You regret last night," he stated flatly, though a giant fist had just slammed him in the belly. The bird of paradise had flown over his head and gifted him with the unpleasant knowledge that Melanie—M. S. Inganforde—wasn't blooming after a night of lovemaking with him. He glanced at the strawberry birthmark on her throat and frowned at the tiny scrapes from his beard near it.

"It's just that we're such opposites, Sloan. Surely you must see that...." she began helplessly, her eyes widening. "Let's talk about this like civilized people. You can have another piece of pie."

"Yoo-hoo! Melanie, honey!" Delilah called just before she swung open the bedroom door.

"Mother!"

"Melanie."

"Sloan," Itty rumbled dangerously, entering the room.

"Itty," Sloan returned. "Nice to see you again."

"Sloan's not presentable," Melanie stated instantly, dragging a rumpled sheet across his hips. "Mother... Itty…please excuse us and make yourself at home…ah…in the living room. I've made coffee."

"This better be good, boy. I don't want my future daughter's reputation damaged. Peaches is sweet, and you'd better not hurt her," Itty rumbled over his shoulder as Delilah pushed him out of the room and quietly closed the door.

"Damn," Sloan muttered, running his hand across his stubble-covered jaw. "How did they get in?"

"Mother has a key to my apartment." Melanie grasped a folded T-shirt from a drawer and pressed jeans from a hanger. She stepped into the bathroom and closed the door just as the doorbell rang.

"Now what?" Sloan asked, prepared now for a flock of birds of paradise flying over his head.

Instead El Lobo and Danielle waited in the living room while Delilah poured coffee and Itty served apple pie. "Hey, Sloan. Good pie," El Lobo said enthusiastically. "Have a racquetball date with Missy. Danielle can't come. So I thought I'd drop her off."

"Hi, Uncle Sloan," Danielle chirped, running to Sloan's arms. He picked her up and met her juicy kiss automatically. "Mr. Itty is taking me and you and Peaches—" she giggled wildly at Melanie's nickname "—and his precious Delilah-babe to a Cards game." Then she kissed him again and Sloan gathered her closer, rubbing her small nose with his until she giggled.

"He's sweet," Delilah said softly, and Sloan turned to see both small women studying him intently.

Delilah's expression was pure delight, but Melanie's was sheer terror. "No," she stated quietly. "No…and double no."

"I'll double your bet, honey. Sloan is a player if ever I saw one," Delilah offered gently, hugging her daughter's shoulders. "Look at him…standing there all rumpled and wary, holding a sweet little girl…. He's perfect."

"Yuck," Melanie returned flatly, looking away. "He sometimes wears a red sock with a green one. You should see his files at the office—bits of napkins, odd names and arrows forming mazes on corporate paper.... There are spaghetti stains on his ties...."

Feeling slightly abused, Sloan glared at her. "I'm a mental player, Mel. It's all upstairs. You play on paper. It takes up time and room. And those are chili dog stains...fast-food service doesn't allow a lot for dripping sauce.... And damn it, *I am color blind.*"

Delilah leaned closer to Melanie, who showed no inclination to soften her attitude. "He needs you, dear," her mother whispered. "Wouldn't he look nice in one of those long nightshirts you like to make for the men of our family? You could make him a tie and color-code his clothes with numbers. Think of him as raw material, dear. You could spend hours organizing his closet alone."

"Wanna play poker, Uncle Sloan?" Danielle offered, waving a package of cards in front of Sloan's face. "El Lobo taught me about a royal flush," she stated proudly. "An ace, king, queen, jack and ten of the same...kind. I like poker better than Go Fish or Old Maid."

Delilah rubbed her hands together and moved to take the little girl from Sloan. "I think we just have time for a fast hand or two. If there's anything I like to do, it's teach a sweet little girl how to play poker. Much more fun than baking cookies or pies. Come here, Danny. Aunt Dee and Mr. Bitty will show you how to play a new game—blackjack."

Melanie glowered at the new dethorned rose bouquet on her file cabinet. She had moved it there to keep from nuzzling the petals and inhaling the fragrance. Monday morning was a time for business, for making lists, for board meetings....

She'd opted to leave her minimizers in their drawer today and choose a light gray suit. The cream blouse flowed against her skin, which seemed extremely sensitized. Tiny muscles within her ached pleasantly at odd moments, and she found herself catching her breath when she sat. She'd taken a long bubble bath the night before, concentrating deeply on the problem with Sloan. Trying to retain a touch of her previous professional look, she'd sprayed and spiked her hair and determinedly inserted the inch-adding lifts into her pumps.

Over hot dogs at the stadium, Sloan had let it slip that Maxine was recovered now and that she would be returning to her post. Tightening his web, he had stated that while Danielle would be included when possible, El Lobo would be happy to baby-sit at odd moments. The playboy pediatrician had developed an empty-nest syndrome. He heard the loud ticks of his biological clock, and outings with Danielle suited his purpose. As his bait, she drew the sort of women who would qualify for potential life-mates.

Melanie studied the roses. Sloan would look wonderful in a cotton nightshirt down to his knees, his hair rumpled and standing out in peaks, his jaw dark with stubble....

She broke the pencil she had been holding. *Sloan Raventhrall,* connoisseur of bodacious amazons, nightshirt candidate...devastating, sweet, gentle lover.

Sloan Raventhrall. Mismatched socks. Horrible filing system. *He knew the secret of her earlobes.*

Melanie stared glumly out the window into the bright sunlight. Sloan had suggested a family-style outing to the zoo. Delilah, Itty and Danielle were excited. Melanie was not.

Nor was she happy about Danielle and Sloan inviting her to go swimming at his health club.

To date, she had not discovered a proper bathing suit. She was too young for the iron-maiden variety, and too curvy for anything less.

Melanie broke another pencil and tapped her pumps on the pedestal beneath her desk.

Sloan, predatory male, had reverted to being the star of Standards Elite. However, at the copier station when no one was around, he had patted her bottom. *She rather liked that fond little pat and was tempted to pat him back.* That would never do. The pats could go on forever. Melanie scowled at the roses.

She knew where the pats could lead.

"Peaches?" Itty asked, hovering uncertainly at her doorway. "Do you have time to talk business?" During this session, Itty agreed with every suggestion, nodded at the proper places and shifted his huge, blocky body constantly, causing his chair to protest in a series of squeaks. Devereau called on the intercom later, asking if Mr. Bitty seemed happy with the transfer from Sloan. Melanie fed Devereau a replay of the session and he was happy.

She was not thrilled with Itty's display of humility.

She'd gotten herself into the roughest game at Elite in order to learn.

Throughout the day, Sloan nodded to her when they passed—except his gaze had moved stealthily, possessively down her suit at the water fountain. Their previous business relationship appeared intact.

By late afternoon, Melanie's list of options for slithering out of the contract she had forced upon Sloan had lengthened. With Maxine back at the housekeeping helm, Danielle should pose little problem.

Danielle called at four o'clock, asking what Melanie would be cooking for supper, and if she could help. She'd used her last coloring book, and she needed a "fresh deck" of cards. Her childish excitement caused Melanie to feel like the worm beneath the grass.

Grass. Melanie thought about a display at a florist shop. Scooping up various notes that the receptionist had deposited on her desk for Sloan during his luncheon with a client, Melanie marched into his office.

Sloan leaned back, sprawling across his huge desk chair, his hair slightly rumpled and his tie loosened as he studied a haphazard collection of *Wall Street Journal* articles and a company brochure for investments. "What's up, Mel?"

As an explanation, she let the clutter of notes from Bambi, Mimi, LaBelle and Juliet fall over his desk. Sloan looked duly uncomfortable as he scooped them into his fist, then crumpled them into the wastepaper basket. "What's up?" he asked again as she slid into the chair in front of his desk.

"We've got to do something about that contract. Under the circumstances, the kindest thing to do would be to explain to Danielle that I am terribly busy.... No, that would hurt her feelings. Sloan, please find some way to not break her little heart when you tell her that we just can't make any further plans as a pseudo-family."

"You're coming over tonight just as you are every evening and weekend, Mel. Unless we're meeting you someplace for convenience sake," he stated firmly. "You're under contract."

She tightened her grip on the chair arms. "You're impossible. In view of what happened, we've got to stop seeing each other—"

Sloan looked at her with deceptively lazy interest—she sensed that predatory streak in him working overtime. "I have worked too hard to break into my career, Sloan. Devereau is thinking of adding another great possibility to my list of clients—Jorge Perez of Rio Products Incorporated. His son, Vinnie, and I have a luncheon appointment on Wednesday."

Sloan snorted, his expression not amused. "Vinnie Perez took the last woman investment counselor down to Rio for dance lessons. His wife is a hot little number who almost shot the counselor with a pearl-handled .22 pistol. Emma hasn't been the same since."

Refusing to be frightened, Melanie straightened her professional pin on her lapel. "It's a good account. Lots of energy and varied investment potential. Perez is—"

"A skirt chaser."

"Look who's talking."

"I'm done with that now, Mel," Sloan stated in a low growl from between the edges of his teeth. "I thought we cleared up that matter this weekend."

A beautiful little thrill of excitement fluttered through Melanie's breast. Pushing Sloan to his limits and rough edges amazed and delighted her. He shed the image of a cool-shark businessman and ignited wonderfully. She crossed her legs, something that M. S. Inganforde never did while in a business situation, and allowed her gray skirt to ride a little higher on her thigh.

She watched with interest as Sloan's eyes darkened. Experimentally she swung her leg, and the material slipped higher. Sloan responded beautifully, watching her legs with a fascination that she found stimulating. Melanie wondered how a black lace slip, such as her mother had worn, would affect Sloan. A sensible granny gown had aroused him—

"Perez is out," he grated slowly.

"Sloan, I'm not taking orders from you," she reminded him sweetly and rose to her feet, aware that his gaze followed her hips out of his office.

The thought pleased her so much that she allowed her body to move into its natural sway.

Sloan cursed softly behind her, causing her to smile. She had never experimented with her femininity, and the thought that she could arouse Sloan by simply walking did wonders for her ego. Melanie hummed as she walked back to her office.

Within seconds, Sloan arrived. He closed the door quietly behind him and stalked toward her desk, eyebrows lowered.

"Perez is out," he repeated quietly, jerking at his tie and unbuttoning the top buttons of his shirt. Low on his throat, beneath the thatch of dark hair covering his chest, were four pink lines. She remembered with a blush the way her fingers had grasped at him just as he poured himself... Melanie closed her eyes and opened them to see Sloan pointing his finger at her. "You're too sweet. You don't realize what a man like that could do."

"Sloan, surely you're not deciding my career moves for me. By managing Perez effectively—and his accounts—I could prove worthy of any investor that Devereau would want to throw my way."

Sloan placed his hands flat on her desk. "I don't want the future mother of my children captured in living skin and being viewed on somebody's television screen. You could be carrying my baby—rather, babies, since my family has twins—right now, Melanie Sue."

Melanie Sue. The name her mother and family used when she misbehaved as a child.

"I am perfectly capable of dealing with Romeos, Sloan," she began after adjusting her professional pin again. Sloan was showing signs of the territorial male flexing his muscles. "If worse comes to worst, don't forget my karate class this spring—"

"You're not acting rational, Melanie. Right now you're pretty confident... Itty's a good account. But Perez is dangerous. *You will not handle his account.*"

For a moment, Melanie stared up at him from behind her large glasses. Then she removed them and folded them slowly. "Are you ordering me to stay away from the Perez account, Raventhrall?"

He glared at her and she noticed the definite primitive flare to his nostrils. "You got it, Inganforde."

She wriggled slightly in her chair, ignoring the pleasantly protesting little muscles she had explored with Sloan during the night. Excitement snaked through her like a high-speed roller coaster. "Because we have had ... an interlude ... does not mean you are telling me—ordering me—how to handle a career that I've worked to develop."

"Damn it, Inganforde. I've just told you that you are not coming close to Vinnie Perez," Sloan roared. "I've got rights."

The silence stretched around the office like a too-tight rubber band. Melanie shivered with the need to vault over her desk and physically attack Sloan. She wanted to throw him over her shoulder. The tense set of his broad shoulders caused her to reconsider. Then there was that muscle shifting beneath the skin covering his jaw; the thrusting angle of that jaw challenged her.... She snapped a pencil, then tossed the pieces on her desk. "You say one word to Devereau about getting me off the Perez account and ..." She didn't complete the sentence, letting him guess at the outcome. "I will not be ruled by a power monger."

"Cute," Sloan muttered, running his hand through his hair. "Now I'm a power monger."

The intercom rang and Georgette MacDougal's cool secretarial voice asked calmly, "M.S.? There seems to be a little disturbance inside your office attracting people in front of your door. Should I hold your calls until your conference is finished?"

Heat spread over Melanie's face. "No. We're finished." She clicked off the intercom button and faced Sloan. "I've worked hard to keep my business profile here at Standards, Raventhrall. Your shouting has drawn a crowd. Please leave."

"Not without this." Then he fitted her against him, taking her mouth in gentle, devastating hunger.

Justin Devereau swirled into her office later, using a minor problem to touch base. "Problems with Raventhrall, M.S.?" he asked gently, settling into her office chair. "Our star player can be difficult at times. Has this layer of steel beneath all that charm. Office gossip has it that you two had a good round of shouting here at the office...."

Melanie tried to muffle the sound of her pencil snapping, and Devereau cleared his throat. "Yes, well. Sometimes laying things on the table serves to get things out in the open where they can be resolved. Raventhrall's got that hungry look lately, like he's up against an account he wants very much."

Devereau leaned closer and spoke quietly. "If it's good for Raventhrall, it's good for Standards Elite. He's like a bird dog scenting out good, ripe quail. Those instincts of his are almost unerring. And unless I miss my guess, he's latched onto something really big. So if he gets a little testy at times, think of the pressure he's under.... Give him a little margin for that tempered steel. I've felt the lash of it myself, although I don't want to let the word get around."

Melanie left early that night to tend her headache. In the two hours she stayed at the apartment, she devoted herself to Danielle. Later, Sloan sat back and sipped the fruit-flavored drink that Danielle had poured for Itty, El Lobo and himself. His niece climbed onto her chair, shuffled the cards and asked Itty, "Cut the cards?"

The three men wore pointy party hats and frowns. Itty shifted his bulk uneasily, then lifted one half the deck from the rest, placing it aside. He glanced at El Lobo, who chewed on a raisin-nut oatmeal cookie and sipped his cherry drink from a toy china cup. Itty glanced at the tiny cup warily, then at his massive, spread hands. "This whole thing ain't natural. Mothers and daughters and little girls are supposed to bond over needlepoint, ain't they? You should see Delilah and Peaches shoot pool. I watched 'em. Like two harks calling each shot. I never got a chance at the table. They were talking all the time about making dressing for the Thanksgiving turkey. Thanksgiving will be at my house," he added proudly. "Delilah is making the dressing. But I'm cooking everything else. Not many women let a man in the kitchen and don't feel threatened."

"Hit me," El Lobo ordered Danielle, perfectly at ease with the situation as she dealt another face-up card. "There's no understanding the female brain. I've studied it from the newborn stage and found every stage of development to be quirky. The rest of the package makes up for the drawbacks."

"Hit me," Sloan said, adjusting Danielle's favorite baby doll and blanket on his lap. While Melanie and Delilah took a night off for a family pajama party, Danielle had been elected to baby-sit for the three men.

Danielle dealt herself a card and grinned slowly, wickedly at each man. Then she yawned prettily and stretched. "Blackjack. An ace and a jack. Will you tuck me and Susie in, Uncle Sloan?"

When he returned to the kitchen, Itty and El Lobo had cleared away the toy china set, replacing it with cans of beer and bowls of peanuts and chips. The first hand of poker, Itty took off his party hat and snarled, "You gotta make Peaches happy, Sloan. If Peaches ain't happy, my sugar pump might skip. I wouldn't like that."

Sloan thought about how he had intended to spend the night in Melanie's four-poster bed. "I've got news for you, Itty. Peaches will be handling the Jorge Perez account. Vinnie is doing the front work. I've checked with my sources and the up-front money is legitimate."

"The hell you say," Itty said, his bushy brows lowering. "Bad news. Jorge knows the score, but Vinnie Perez doesn't take no from broads. Peaches is just a little, sweet kid. She wouldn't know what the likes of Perez can do. Jerk her off the account. Tell her what's what."

While Sloan studied his cards, El Lobo took a deep breath and said, "Three cards, Itty.... The thing with the female brain, gentlemen, is that you never, never tell a woman what to do. My guess is that our chum here has made that fatal mistake on the day following his first...ah...romantic encounter with M. S. Inganforde. He is now in the proverbial doghouse."

"She called me a 'power monger,'" Sloan muttered, feeling very fragile. He studied his full house bleakly and ripped off his party hat. Not so many hours ago, Melanie Sue had called him "darling."

Itty stared at Sloan and blinked. "Damn.... 'Power-monger'.... Boy, you *have* to make yourself more appetizing. Take lessons or something. Learn how to treat the ladies. Maybe El Lobo here can refer you to a charm school."

Later, Sloan lay in his bed, arms folded behind his head. He nudged a stuffed, long-eared dog off his bed and thought about cuddling M. S. Inganforde. Things weren't going smoothly in the nymph-capturing business.

Itty was correct. He had to make himself more... *appealing* as potential husband material.

"Perez is out," he repeated to the shadows, drawing his favorite pillow into the spoon of his body. It had been a long, exhausting day, and Danielle's hot dogs were beginning to rumble in his stomach. He didn't like being called a power monger by the woman he loved. Nor did he like thinking about Perez.

Perez might have the account Melanie wanted, but Sloan had a secret weapon—Danielle.

On Tuesday, Sloan foraged for recipes. Melanie would be working late at the office, and he wanted her to come home to a good home-cooked meal, thus demonstrating his house-husband skills. He left work early, picked up the necessary groceries and enlisted Danielle's help.

Melanie arrived, weary and hungry, to find dinner waiting for her. Sloan took her briefcase and coat, slipped her
half a glass of wine and asked her to relax and enjoy the
stock-market reports on the television. He delicately skipped
the welcoming kiss after Melanie's forbidding frown, then
shuttled into the kitchen to put the finishing touches on the
candle-lit meal.

Danielle dominated dinner, chirping along happily, while
Melanie praised the salad she had prepared.

"This is nice, isn't it?" Sloan ventured tentatively, while
he grated fresh Parmesan cheese over Melanie's spaghetti.

She stared at him warily, then pushed her glasses higher
on her nose. "Very nice. Thank you."

Sloan recoiled a little at the frosty tone.

"I made the salad," Danielle boasted proudly. "Uncle
Sloan made the spa-spaghetti."

Melanie bent to kiss his niece. "The dinner is delicious
and such a nice thought. Thank you."

While Danielle beamed, Sloan cleared his throat. He
hoped for a little petting and received a dark, searing stare.

Later Sloan cleaned the kitchen while Melanie and Danielle planted a square of grass that required trimming and
watering. He placed the kettle he'd used to cook spaghetti
and the sauce pot in the oven, making a mental note to ask
Maxine to wash them, then scouted Melanie's intent expression. Bent over the grass plot that would be Danielle's
special project to grow, Melanie was perfect—except for that
blind spot about Perez and her career.

Testing the moody waters delicately, Sloan ventured,
"Say, you know I've never noticed before, but this place
could use some plants. Maybe...ah...what do you think
about African violets?" he asked, remembering the spray
across Melanie's window. "There's a greenhouse that's open
late—why don't we go shopping?"

Danielle clapped her hands and began chattering about
Venus flytraps. Melanie turned slowly, the muted light

catching the gold in her hair. She seemed to grow six inches as she faced him. "You are banned from our shopping trips until otherwise advised, Raventhrall. When we want you, we shall invite you. This is a ladies-only trip."

Sloan wasn't used to being dismissed, much less by his ladylove. "You're not going out tonight—without me," he stated firmly, secure that Melanie would agree with his reasoning. "It could be dangerous."

She smiled and adjusted the barrette in Danielle's braid. "I agree. It's Tuesday night. Danielle and I are working on our coloring books and cutting out dolls. Maybe play a good round of jacks. We'll put plant shopping on our Saturday or Sunday list. That way we'll have more time. We'll go on a safari."

"Lists," Sloan muttered darkly, taking a step toward her. He wanted his mouth on hers, needed to feel the soft, welcoming warmth parting to him. He wanted her snuggled against him, exploring their new relationship. "The safari part sounds good."

He had the satisfaction of Melanie's eyes opening wider, swallowing his image as he loomed over her. Then Danielle tugged on his slacks. He automatically lifted her into his arms, and she stroked his taut jaw. "I don't mind, Uncle Sloan. I've never been on a saf-safari before. I'd rather stay with my new grass, anyway. Melanie says that it should sprout tonight."

He blinked. When Danielle's whims were easily rerouted, things were definitely serious. M. S. Inganforde was a dangerous woman. "I'm going to El Lobo's," he stated carefully, escaping to a safer territory.

Eight

Melanie's Wednesday business luncheon with Vinnie proceeded on schedule. Over Gino's succulent salad and crusty rolls, Vinnie laid out the possibilities of varying investments, environmentally related products with a modest rate of returns. His gold tooth added charm to his dark, thin face; his narrow, small eyes skimmed her gray business suit and explored the white blouse.

Vinnie explained carefully about the Perez investments and how important it was that someone fresh handle their accounts at Standards. The Perez family had selected Standards because of the company's impeccable, classy clients. Listening carefully to Vinnie's outline for profits, and taking notes, Melanie barely noticed the rather bulky men settling around their table.

Her napkin slipped a little over her thigh and she reached to adjust it. Vinnie's hand rested beneath the material and slid away when she frowned slightly. He smiled and nodded to one of the men who immediately summoned the waiter to pour more wine into Melanie's glass. "I never have wine at lunch, Mr. Perez. Keeping a cool head is something we know how to do at Standards."

Vinnie smiled, his gold tooth glittering. "Maybe just this once, eh? Now, what were you saying about Alamo Paper Products—they're recycling, right? Good sturdy investment potential?"

Excited about tucking the Perez account in her files, Melanie explained the various growth ratios of potential companies that might interest the Perez family. She barely noticed Vinnie's nod and the waiter pouring a third glass of wine.

When the ravioli arrived, Vinnie leaned back in his chair and eyed the prim cotton blouse she had opened because of the room's heat. "I'd really like to get some things settled today, Melanie. Offices make me nervous—tight little places like the joint...ah, elevators with dead air, you know. How about finishing our business at my suite?"

"Oh, heavens, no. I couldn't—"

"You got a boyfriend or something that would object to your business with a client?" Vinnie sneered slightly. "Look, I don't waste time with companies that can't be flexible when there's big cash involved. Maybe we should call it quits now...."

She could feel her victory sliding away, and blinked as Vinnie refilled her glass and rested his arm on the back of her chair. He toyed with a curl at the back of her neck. "We can do business. I just don't like interruptions."

Melanie glanced at his eyes and found them probing her blouse. While Sloan's sexy stare down her body caused her to feel cherished, Vinnie's leer drew a cold shiver. Her breasts quivered, and Vinnie's eyes pinned them as he leered wider. His hand ran lightly, damply across her knees beneath the table, squeezing each one. "Come on, Melanie, loosen up. You're a pro. You must know that not all business is settled in an office. I got phone calls waiting for me at the suite. You can make your pitch better without all this noise.''

She eased away from his hand. It followed as she nervously sipped the iced drink. Vinnie leaned closer, flicking her earlobe. *Sloan's favorite earlobe.*

Over one of the bulky men leering at her, Melanie spotted Sloan, El Lobo and Danielle behind a barrage of ferns.

She couldn't allow the situation to get out of hand. She was a professional businesswoman with a potential client— Vinnie's hand slid higher on her thigh. Scooting to the edge of her chair, she drank the filled glass of wine quickly.

Slightly dizzy, she glanced longingly at the threesome chatting beyond the restaurant's foliage. Vinnie rose suddenly, and the four big, blocky men got to their feet, moving in to surround him as he circled Melanie's upper arm and drew her to her feet.

''Oh, dear, Mr. Perez,'' she managed, protesting just as one of the men picked up her briefcase.

''Take it easy, sugar. Don't make no scene,'' Vinnie ordered, slipping his arm around her waist to draw her against him.

She skidded slightly, digging her pumps into the lush carpeting, but the men moved her along as though she were a bubble on a stream. She wanted Sloan's strong arms closing around her, her head tucked firmly beneath his chin....

''Mama!'' Danielle called, waving at her over the potted plants. Melanie caught sight of Sloan's dark, predatory expression as he rose slowly to his feet. El Lobo, another tall man, rose like a shadow beside him. Slightly faint, Melanie thought of Southern belles and dueling gentlemen—except Vinnie didn't fit the gallant image. She changed the image to the Green Berets or the Texas Rangers rescuing a woman in distress. While she considered methods of handling the situation as a professional businesswoman, capable of dealing with dangerous challenges, Danielle's voice carried through the restaurant. ''Mama, wait.''

"Mama?" Vinnie asked sharply as Danielle burrowed between the legs of the burly men to Melanie. She held Melanie's hand tightly, glaring up at Vinnie.

"Mama," Danielle stated possessively as Sloan and El Lobo moved toward them. A third bulky man rose from his table, tossed down a few bills and turned, moving toward her. Itty's lowered brows signaled a full-scale war. In her panic, Melanie realized she had never seen anything so endearing as the three tall men approaching her.

Danielle glowered up at Vinnie. "Take your hands off my mama. She's mine!"

"Hi, honey," Sloan's cool voice said beyond one of the men blocking her view. The too-soft, low tone caused the hair at the back of her neck to stand up. "Are you feeling all right?"

"Uh, I'm just having lunch with Mr. Perez—business." She wanted to run to Sloan, but Vinnie anchored her to his side. She noted with satisfaction that the goons did not dismiss Sloan easily.

Sloan met one of the goon's eyes evenly. The stare held and darkened before the man seemed to shrink. He moved aside slightly, leaving an opening for Sloan to approach Vinnie and his wilting prisoner. "Take your mother's briefcase, Danielle," Sloan said between his teeth, moving closer to Melanie. "I think she's ready to go home now. At four months' pregnant she really should rest after being up all night with your baby brother. Don't worry, honey. Grandma will pick up the other two children at day school."

Melanie struggled for control; somehow she had to manage the bad situation she had created. "Uh...darling...meet Mr. Perez, a business acquaintance...."

"Mr. Perez," Sloan said, his teeth showing slightly behind his tightly drawn-back lips. "My wife seems to have wilted a little this afternoon. Sometimes she bites off more than she can chew... it's a symptom of her pregnancy."

He smiled coldly at Vinnie, and Melanie stared up, dazed by the tough, fearless expression of a man who would fight for his ladylove. "You don't mind if I see my wife back to the office, do you, Mr. Perez?"

The goon carrying Melanie's briefcase grunted when Danielle kicked his shin. "Give me my mama's briefcase *now,*" she ordered relentlessly. "My favorite colorbook is in there and my jacks."

"Vinnie?" the goon asked pleadingly as Danielle eyed his other shin.

"Ah, sh—" Vinnie cursed, releasing Melanie. "Do it. Let's go. You're sharp, baby. You got the account. I'll send my business manager into the office next week. Good luck with the kids." Sloan's strong arm slipped to support her before she wilted to the carpeting's huge flowers. She wondered vaguely if she'd hit the spaghetti stain in the center of the blooming rose pattern.

"I could have handled the situation," Melanie protested later while Sloan ushered her inside the Standards building. Tucking her against him, he swept them inside one slot of the revolving glass door. "Vinnie was just testing—"

Over the top of her head, Sloan's hard chin shifted. She thought she heard the grating of teeth as he drew her closer. "Sure he was."

"Poor Danielle. You didn't have to drag her into the scenario."

"'Poor Danielle' plotted the whole thing. Itty offered an alternative...he wanted to rip out Perez's throat. Which one would you prefer?" Sloan asked grimly.

While Melanie foraged for an adequate reply, Sloan nudged her into the Standards lobby, nodded to the main receptionist and said, "Touch of upset stomach. Inganforde could have the flu. I'm taking her straight to her office. Get her appointment sheet from Georgette and cancel them, okay?"

"I'm fine, Sloan," she managed as another wave of dizziness slid through her, forcing her to grip his arm and stare helplessly up at his face. Another image replaced the Texas Ranger and Green Beret one—this time she sensed pure possessive male fury, or lava boiling in a volcano, ready to stream down the mountain.... She decided that she'd wait until she could deal with her upset stomach and strange, light-headed feeling. Standards' jade carpeting loomed very close as Sloan grimly eased her into the elevator.

Within moments, she was settled on Sloan's lap behind his office's locked doors. He adjusted the cool cloth across her forehead and grimly urged her to drink coffee. "I'd take you home, but the M. S. Inganforde image is that she's always in control, always at the helm and ready for new juicy accounts, right?" he asked tightly.

"You're upset," she said finally after nestling into the hard cove of his body and savoring the way his jaw settled protectively on the top of her head.

"Eat those damn crackers," he snapped, flipping through his messages.

"It was nice of you and El Lobo to take Danielle to lunch," she said, trying to divert Sloan's temper. He needed soothing, and she just couldn't summon the right words.

"A novice player like you should know better than to have wine, especially Chianti—"

"What do you mean, 'novice player'?" she asked, attempting to leave his lap. Another wave of dizziness forced her back under his chin. "I've been at Standards for five years, and my degree in business—"

"I mean, dear heart," Sloan answered as he dipped a washcloth in the glass of ice water on his desk, "that you were being set up for an afternoon in Vinnie's favorite play parlor. You could have been the star of one of his famous movies."

"I've never taken good pictures," Melanie returned, horrified at Sloan's grim implications. "I look chunky—"

"Curvy. The word is voluptuous and hot...very hot," Sloan muttered, handing her another saltine cracker. "You'd look like dynamite on Vinnie's black satin sheets."

"How did you know where we were lunching?" she asked, nibbling on the cracker and trying to fit together the pieces of the scenario.

"Itty's tipoff. He tailed you to Gino's, said you were being set up. Didn't like the idea of his future stepdaughter being used for X-rated viewing material. He read me the riot act for letting you—repeat, *letting* you—have dinner with Vinnie alone."

He jerked open a drawer and lifted out a black tin painted with an Oriental design. She closed her eyes, trying to stop her world from spinning.

Suddenly Sloan's jaw moved and a *crunch-crunch* sound echoed through her aching head. "What are you doing, Sloan?" she asked cautiously, afraid to move. Her stomach hadn't stabilized.

"Chinese fortune cookies," he explained, unrolling a small slip of paper with his fingers. "When faced with a major problem, I resort to elementary research.... You, M. S. Inganforde, are a major problem."

"What is your fortune?" she asked, as the *crunch-crunch* continued and Sloan shifted slightly, kissing her forehead.

"The first one says, 'Beware of soft, light, beautiful objects that you desire. They could be dangerous to your health.' The second one says, 'A woman you know will create a special glow in your life. Treat her gently.' I don't feel like treating you gently, Melanie Sue," he said slowly, gathering her closer. "You seem to have forgotten who you belong to."

Beneath her cheek, his heartbeat increased. "Now, Sloan..."

"Didn't anyone ever tell you to leave slugs like Vinnie in the garbage?" he continued, drawing in a deep breath and resettling the cool cloth over her forehead.

"Sloan..." she sniffed, fighting off the tears burning behind her lids. She didn't want to cry, didn't want to cling to Sloan's solid body for comfort. He just felt so right in her lurching seas, so warm and tender. "I was so frightened...." She'd never been truly frightened before, not since her favorite kitten was trapped high on a maple tree in her family's backyard.

He inhaled sharply, his muscles tensing. "Don't cry, Melanie. We'll get through this. All you have to do is stay put in your office until five o'clock. Georgette will tell everyone not to disturb you, that you're working on a special project. She'll field your messages to me. While you were in my private washroom, I explained that you weren't feeling well... that you didn't want to break your perfect attendance at Standards. Georgette is tough and experienced. She can deflect Devereau like a piece of fluff."

Melanie tried not to sniff, managing to swallow though her throat had tightened with emotion. "You sound like you're planning a rescue mission.... Oh, drat and double drat...."

Sloan settled back to rock her gently, placing his warm hand behind her knees to draw her fully onto his lap. "Take it easy, sweetheart. Even M. S. Inganforde, professional woman, can make a mistake."

Allowing herself to be cuddled and petted, Melanie stroked Sloan's broad chest and slipped her palm just inside his shirt. She stroked the crisp hair and warm skin covering his steely muscles and enjoyed the sensation of Sloan almost purring. In the pleasant afternoon sunlight shafting through the blinds, she treasured Sloan's intimate, caring nature. "What was she like, Sloan?"

"Mmm?" Sloan almost purred, his chin nestling over her head. He nuzzled her curls, sniffing appreciatively. "She who?"

"Your wife. Are we alike?"

He jerked upright, almost unseating her. "Gad, no."

She stroked his chest, toying with his nipple, which responded by becoming nicely taut. "You could tell me about her.... I mean, was she...attractive? Uh...was she good...?"

"I'm not in the mood for this now, M.S.," Sloan stated flatly, lifting her to her feet. He jerked her between his knees and swished the damp, cold cloth around her face and throat. He thrust it into her fingers, then placed her hand at the back of her neck. "Hold it."

Sloan fastened her blouse button that had loosened, tucked her blouse into her waistband. He scowled at her hose, which had huge runs. Melanie stared at the ruined hose and sniffed. She distinctly remembered Vinnie's long nails probing her knee. She blinked, and a huge tear strolled down her cheek to splatter on Sloan's dark hand. He stared at the damp spot for a minute, then drew her head down to his. His kiss was everything, slightly hungry, tender, rough—a lover's kiss amid troubled times.

"What will our children say? All four of them," she asked in a shaky attempt to right her slanting world.

He patted her tummy, splaying his hand over it to rub it gently. "Five, counting Junior here."

"Good Lord, Sloan. Five children and a career, too? I must be Supermom."

"Don't forget, M.S.," Sloan whispered tenderly, running his finger across her damp lashes, "I can be your friend and your lover, a Supermom's perfect life-mate. Think about it."

"We'd fight," she ventured as he unsnapped her garters and began drawing off her ruined hose. "We're not compatible. Your files are a mess. And today you're wearing a green sock and a red one.... Where is Danielle?"

"Itty took her to his place. Delilah is teaching her and Itty how to play pool. Itty's game needs help. No spin on the ball." Bent over his task, Sloan stroked her thigh gently as he lifted her left foot to his knee. "Up."

She braced her hand on his shoulder, watched with interest as he reached into a drawer and rummaged through it to extract an assortment of hose. Wrapping his fingers around her ankle, he read the labels, selected a package and opened it with his teeth. "Sloan, why do you have stockings in your desk drawer?" she asked carefully.

He tossed the empty wrapper into his trash. "Women clients appreciate a counselor who can supply hose. It's a good investment in trust and saves them the embarrassment of wearing torn hose." Within minutes, he had replaced her stockings and stood her upright while he smoothed her hair with a brush extracted from her purse.

Melanie stood perfectly still while Sloan administered his finishing touches. Like an artist, he concentrated on the tumbling curls at her temples, then reached for Danielle's gold barrette in his pocket. He drew back the curls and clasped them. "You've done this before," she said.

"I have a sister. One learns to survive." He extracted a small tube of toothpaste and a toothbrush from a box. "Use my washroom, honey. Take your time." Then he patted her on the bottom and drew her mouth down for another kiss. "You'll make it, Inganforde. You're tough."

"You're truly sweet, Sloan," she said after returning from the private bathroom. She felt moderately restored and uncertain how to handle Sloan. She approached his chair slowly and noted how he watched her—like a man who was very, very angry. They shared a long, gauging look into each other's eyes. There was steel and something soft, infinitely warm in the depths of Sloan's dark brown eyes. She caressed his cheek, smoothing the line between his brows caused by the last few hours of tension. "You were worried."

"Damn right, I was. You could have been Vinnie's latest cream-filled cupcake," he said unevenly. "If he so much as calls you . . ."

She knew better than to argue. "That was quite a sight. El Lobo, Itty and you storming Vinnie's goons. They could have hurt you.... Promise me you won't be so daring in the future."

"I wasn't the one in danger, Mel," he reminded her in a low, soft voice. "And you'd better not confuse the issue with gratitude. I want you wearing my ring and in my bed because you want to be there, not because you're grateful."

Later, when Melanie was back in her own office, Georgette buzzed her. "Sorry. Devereau at high noon. Sloan seems to be in a snit, and the old boy is asking questions about his star player. Couldn't stop him."

Within seconds, Devereau tapped at her office door and entered her office. He dropped a file on her desk. "Everything we have on Jorge Perez, *your* client. Congratulations, M.S. He was impressed by your knowledge of our business."

Without a break, Devereau continued, "Our star player is having strange moods. Today he's a little testy. It's probably the pressure of that big, juicy account he's been working on. See if you can't help him out a little, eh, Inganforde? You know, give it the old Standards Elite try for a fellow teammate. Help Raventhrall fine-tune his strategies. You could learn something in the process."

At five o'clock Sloan jerked open her office door. "I'm going home with you, Mel. Danielle is staying the night with Itty and Delilah. Your mother is thrilled. Itty's not so happy. Your car needed a muffler, so I called Petey's Garage to come pick it up."

"You're being a little heavy-handed, Sloan," Melanie reminded him as she maneuvered through the revolving door. "People will talk."

He shot her a dark look. "Don't," he ordered tightly. "Just don't."

Too weak to protest, Melanie allowed Sloan to grimly lift her into his black beast and soar through Kansas City's chilly concrete maze to her apartment building. "Sit still," he ordered her as she began to slide out the passenger door.

Melanie gauged the long distance down to the street puddles and decided to obey.

At her apartment, Sloan took the keys from her hand and opened the door.

She cleared her throat. "You're angry."

"You could say that." Sloan nudged her into the dark apartment and flipped on her lights. Then he stood back in the shadows of the hallway.

She cleared her throat again. "Would you like to come in for tea and a sandwich...I'm just famished, and you could have the last of the family apple pie—"

"No thanks, not tonight. I have a headache." There in the dim light of the hallway, Sloan's face resembled a grim granite carving. Melanie wanted him to hold her, to cuddle her and snuggle with her in her four-poster, erasing the day's events forever.

He watched her flounder for an excuse. "Ah, thank you for today, Sloan."

"Sure."

"Ah...you were right about Vinnie. Are you sure you wouldn't like that apple pie? I could warm it, and it's delicious with cream...."

He couldn't be bought. She knew it, but offered anyway, testing him. The line between his brows hadn't softened, and she sighed tiredly. "You're going to be difficult about this, aren't you?"

"In a word—yes," he answered coldly.

She leaned against the doorframe, feeling much like a wilted daisy. "Oh, my."

"Yes, oh, my. You're over your head, Inganforde. That's why you've got the weekend off from Danielle. I'd advise you to do some serious thinking." Then he cupped her chin, clamped an arm around her waist to lift her to him.

His kiss was undisguised hunger; more savage than ever before, it tasted of loneliness and despair, of eagerness and the future. There with her feet inches from the floor, Sloan fitted her against the arousal of his hips, kissed her and petted her until she vibrated with longing. Her fingertips dug into his suit, her mouth fitted hungrily to his demanding one.

If she could just drag him into her four-poster ... or even her apartment....

He nuzzled her hair for a moment, inhaling the fragrances, then whispered coarsely into her ear, "If you want me, Mel, you're going to have to come and get me. I won't be easy. I'll want the whole enchilada."

With that, he lowered her to her feet, turned her toward her apartment and patted her bottom, nudging her inside. The door closed silently behind her.

Melanie stood shaking with desire in the darkness. She wanted to tear after him, drag him back to her apartment and have her way with him. She blinked, rage throbbing at her suddenly. *Come and get me.... I won't be easy....*

He made her sound like a bird dog after quail, a hungry tiger on the hunt.... A wicked, unfulfilled, sexy woman who loved a difficult man. She groaned, fighting the bodacious images of the women who were drawn to Sloan. Now she knew why—he was a delectable man, a compassionate, loving, sweet, dear man who could set women on fire. How could she compete with the bodacious man hunters?

Come and get me.... I won't be easy....

"Drat and double drat."

Sloan lay in the dark, the neon lights of the city flickering through his window. This afternoon he'd almost squashed Vinnie Perez like the cockroach he was. Dangling like a doll against Vinnie's stiletto body, Melanie was clearly frightened and helpless, her expression like that of a child who had just been told there was no Santa Claus.

He scowled at Danielle's teddy bear who shared his womanless bed. Melanie still slightly believed in Santa Claus and the Easter Bunny; he'd seen her expression of delight at the office parties.

Gambling with foreign investments in unstable economies was exciting; gambling with Melanie's love was extremely dangerous. Added to that, the growth ratio of her previously untapped sensuality could lead to disaster—with other men.

He inhaled sharply, remembering the husky, sultry, beckoning tone of her voice as she clung tightly to him. *Oh, Sloan... darling....*

He shifted to one side, drawing his favorite pillow into the spoon of his body and caressing it gently.

If he made one wrong move in this takeover plot, he could lose his nymph, his ladylove, his wifey-to-be and the mother of his children.

Sloan hugged the pillow tighter, staring grimly at the neon lights.

M. S. Inganforde, an in-charge executive business-woman, possessed a layer of steel. She'd fought against Standards's male-dominated strata and had forged a measure of respect from the upper ranks. She'd built a career she badly wanted. It was a part of her that Sloan didn't want endangered. He wanted her to slug out her top performance, yielding nothing to him as a professional.

They'd worked well together in the past, and in transferring Itty's ownership. Their private relationship—their love—could and would have the same mutual respect.

There was bending and blending in their work patterns; he wanted as much from their love.

Melanie was not fully committed because she hadn't done the running to date. Leaving her out on the proverbial limb would allow her to invest in a serious relationship.

Ladyloves weren't easy to trap... not the lifetime breed. Leaving Melanie on her doorstep, her blue eyes darkened by passion, was worse than difficult. It had left him with aches that could not be eased by a long, cold shower.

He nuzzled the soft pillow with his cheek, longing for Melanie's pale, silky, flower-scented skin.

Sloan wanted her love, not her gratitude. Sitting back and waiting for her to decide she loved him wasn't easy for a player. Loving Melanie was like putting together a well-balanced investor's portfolio. One had to balance the percentages....

Melanie sniffed into her rumpled lace handkerchief. She had thoroughly bathed, washing away Vinnie's slimy grip, and had settled down to resolve *the problem with Sloan.*

Sloan's cold, forbidding expression could not be removed as easily. He was hurt, his delicate male ego needed stroking and soothing, and she ached to pet him. There was that angry muscle sliding along his jaw that needed tending and the taut muscles standing out in relief on his tanned throat that needed kisses.

She groaned, yanking her favorite pillow against her and gently clawing her nails down the pink-and-cream stripes, the way she wanted to touch Sloan to drive him over the edge.

She would never forget his expression as she dangled from Vinnie's arm. A passionate warrior claiming his woman....

Melanie dug her nails into the pillowcase. She could be just as fierce, just as passionate.... To date, she just hadn't had the proper material with which to practice.

Nine

Itty carefully eased his bulk into Melanie's office chair, and Melanie wanted to remove the frightened, cornered-animal look in his eyes. After making priority lists this weekend, she'd decided to start out Monday morning by making Itty more at ease. She purposefully tossed a crumpled paper to the floor and another one into the hoop attached to her trash basket. A tin of fortune cookies rested in her desk drawers.

Sloan had passed her in the hallway with little or no notice, except when he'd asked Danielle, Delilah and Itty to lunch on Friday. Then, of course, he was obligated to ask Delilah's daughter.

Polite, aloof and intensely desirable, Sloan avoided any contact with her hand—or other parts—during lunch. Danielle chattered away happily, hugging the new coloring book that Melanie had given her. Her grass was growing nicely and her Uncle Sloan lost regularly at poker and blackjack. Uncle El Lobo would go shopping with her on Saturday afternoon, but she had to smile and be nice to the women he might invite to have strawberry milk shakes with them.

Oak leaves swirled against Melanie's window in brilliant October yellows and oranges, then fell to the ground.

She hadn't been invited to the poker and pool fest at Itty's mansion, and decided it was just as well. She needed to think about her life and her loves.

She'd spent the weekend baking and freezing apple dumplings and making lengthy lists. Sunday evening at eleven o'clock she gave up trying to sleep, keeping fresh for her Itty project, and began laying out material on her floor, snipping at it while she thought about Sloan. At one o'clock Monday morning, she jerked her minimizers from her sacheted drawer and began snipping them in half. She made shopping lists of practical business underwear, then added a separate list of sexy, male-interest-getting lingerie. A lacy black slip headed that list. She reorganized her business underwear list, deciding that she would wear lace under good sturdy business fabrics. In a stroke of brilliance, she added bikini panties and Parfum Bon Soir, a sensuous, elusive musk designed to attract the most reluctant male.

He was a true gentleman, her passionate warrior. When he could have taken advantage of her scattered defenses, he did not.

Sloan had presented her with a challenge that she couldn't pass up. She hummed while she sewed the brown-and-cream-striped material, fashioning the nightshirt. He would look wonderful, rumpled and sexy.

Pillow-hugging at midnight was a sport she did not intend to continue.

In front of her desk, Itty cleared his throat and shifted uneasily in his chair. "Are you having trouble, Peaches?" he asked nervously. "'Cause if you are, just ask, and I'll take care of it."

Melanie snapped her pencil in two, focusing on the task before her. Itty jumped when the pencil pieces hit her desk.

When she walked to her office door and closed it, Itty's small eyes followed her. They widened as she sat, kicked off her shoes and propped her feet on her desk. Slacks were wonderful, she decided instantly, leaning back to make herself more comfortable. They gave her a feeling of power. Teamed with a dark brown turtleneck, a heavy gold chain and a darker blazer, she retained a pert, businesslike image.

She clicked on the remote for the recently installed television set and flipped through the channels to a ball game. "They won't make the World Series . . . too bad. Bernacetti's quite a slugger. A real long-ball threat," she offered, drawing a sack of unshelled peanuts from her drawer. She cut the sack and poured the nuts into a bowl.

Itty stared at the bowl, then at the television. "What's the scam, Peaches?"

Melanie cracked a peanut, dropped the waste into her basket and munched thoughtfully. "It occurs to me, Itty, that you don't know the real me. We need a good relationship—understanding that we're both players with the same goals—revving up your portfolio. If you can spare the time, let's work on better understanding each other this morning. Let's focus on what you want, and how I can get it for you."

"Damn," Itty muttered softly, skillfully snapping a peanut shell in half with one hand and flipping the nut into his mouth. He tossed the shells back into the bowl and Melanie struggled to conceal her grimace.

She reached into the ice bucket under her desk and lifted a frosty root beer bottle out, offering it to Itty. His eyes lit up. "Root beer, the old-fashioned bottled kind. My favorite," he said, jerking the lid off with one twist of his hands and guzzling deeply. He ran the back of his hand across his mouth. "Sloan and I are going to brew the stuff in my basement."

Melanie mentally patted herself on the back, then stealthily checked the list on her desk. Jerking a deck of cards from her drawer, she began to deal. "Mogul Enterprises and Centipede Electronics stock went up. You were right to invest in them."

"Yeah," Itty growled, opening another peanut with one hand and flipping the nut into his mouth. He picked up his cards, studied them and tugged open the knot in his flower-splattered tie. He placed three cards on the center of the table, studying the replacement that Melanie quickly dealt to him. "Sloan didn't think much of Vertigo stock."

Melanie discarded three cards and dealt herself another set, studying them as she wiggled her toes. "Vertigo's a family-owned company. It's splitting at the seams... bigger companies are hovering around it like vultures. We could wait until the feathers settle, then if the takeover looks good, we could move on that stock."

"Vertigo makes those cute little black slips that my sugar likes," Itty threw back stubbornly before his eyes widened and he stared at Melanie with an expression of pure horror.

"They put together a good-grade slip," Melanie said as they continued to play. She wanted to place Itty at ease. "I'm going to buy one myself."

"Yeah." Itty was silent for a moment, looked up at a pitched ball on the television and muttered, "Slider. Hernandez will never hit it."

"Two to one he'll knock it into the bleachers... left field."

"Nah. You're on."

Hernandez caught the slider with the end of his bat and sent it into the bleachers past left field. The fans screamed. Itty stared at Melanie "This ain't right, somehow.... It's... it's indecent."

She grinned, flipped a shelled peanut high into the air and caught it in her mouth. "Mom taught me everything I know."

"Damn and double damn."

"You see, Itty, after my stepfather passed away, Mother and I had to take up the slack of raising my baby brother. We wanted him to know the basics. My aunt Mabel is a champion pool shark. Aunt Petunia is wonderful at poker, especially stud."

That night, Melanie warmed her apple dumplings and served them to Sloan and Danielle with liberal dollops of whipped cream. Danielle and she worked together at the kitchen table, cutting out doll dresses, which the girl played with when Melanie tried desperately to work from her briefcase.

Sloan hadn't noticed her new image, though he did pad back into the kitchen for another heated apple dumpling.

When she finished tucking Danielle in with the story of Sleeping Beauty, Sloan met her at the bedroom door. In the shadows, he looked down at her so intensely that she blushed. "How are you feeling?" he asked softly, stroking her earlobe with the tip of his finger.

She shifted nervously against the wall, suddenly very aware of how much she wanted to fling herself at Sloan and take him there on the carpeting.

"Great," she managed in a soft, husky tone as the muscles of her thighs began to heat and weaken. "How are you feeling?"

Sloan's hand curved around her neck to draw her to his kiss. "You're driving me nuts," he stated gently, brushing his lips across hers. "Jessica is collecting Danielle...she misses her. Then you're moving in with me. You can do your running where you're safe from the Vinnie Perezes of the world."

Melanie blinked, feeling slightly as though she had stepped over the edge of a cliff. "I can?"

He drew her against him and tucked his chin over her head, smoothing her back with long, elegant, possessive strokes. "Sweetheart, it's the best thing."

"It is?" Melanie wondered absently how Sloan could be so delicious, appealing... and oblivious to the mistake he was about to make.

He rocked her gently, kissing the top of her head. "Think about it. Make a few lists...."

Melanie's hands rose to wedge inches between Sloan's chest and her head. "You're telling me what is the best thing for me? For us?" she asked carefully. "Just like that?"

"Mmm." Sloan kissed her cheek, pressing her hips against him. "I've decided that you don't have to come and get me."

"I don't?" Melanie tried to control her rising anger. Sloan may treat her well in their business relationship, but he needed a lesson about their personal matters.... *Two* people set the rules for a romance.

His finger traced her lips, his eyes glowing sensually. "Huh-uh."

"You mean live together and then I can do my running to get you *and* be safe from other men?" When he nodded, she moved out of his arms cautiously. "In other words—if I understand you correctly—you are tucking me under your wing.... I'll think about it."

"You do that," he agreed, drawing her close for a long, heart-stopping kiss.

"Have you noticed the change in Inganforde?" Devereau asked thoughtfully as he watched Nick Landis hover around Melanie.

Sloan crushed a packaged fortune cookie in his fist and tossed the cellophane-wrapped crumbs into his trash basket. He leaned back in his chair and rocked. Melanie's fond little pats on his backside were unnerving. While he appreciated her soft curves beneath his palm, he was uncertain if return play was justified. He'd never thought of his tush as a recipient of feminine enjoyment and possession. Melanie's new attitude concerning his tush chafed his assurance as a male who dominated a relationship with a sweet nymph. That small, little hand patting his backside rattled and challenged him. "I noticed."

"M.S. is turning into a female power monger. Did you see the way she asserted herself at the conference? Stepped right out there and lectured on the investment possibilities of Butterman's New Heart Valve . . . an iffy deal." Devereau's tone lowered as he said slowly, "She must be working out at the gym. Changing her figure and hair. Women do that sort of thing just when you get comfortable with one image. They are a shifty commodity. Landis seems impressed, so does Miles and Rodney. . . . She's got a special friend, though. Sends her flowers."

Sloan stared glumly at Melanie's round, bodacious hips as Devereau swept on down the hallway. Landis made lists, his files in immaculate order. His business profile exactly matched Melanie's. The two of them could organize and file in ecstasy.

You'll have to come and get me. . . . A sensuous, delectable commodity, Melanie could possibly explore her new femininity with another man. Perhaps she would pat another man's tush with that same air of possession.

Who the hell did he think he was, waiting for Melanie to "come and get" him?

Just then, she turned and stared straight at him. The look held and heated, riveting Sloan to his chair. His toes curled within his blue sock and his brown one as she ignored Landis and began walking toward his office. "How's it going?" she asked at his doorway.

Sloan took in the line of her skirt, flowing down her long legs. "Pretty good. How's it going with you?"

Melanie's gaze touched his unbuttoned collar, his loosened tie, and skimmed his legs. The shade of her eyes darkened to indigo, and her expression reminded him of his delectable, hungry, shy nymph. The impact on Sloan's body sent him straining against his slacks. "Great. I've got a new Agnes and Lurpy coloring book."

"I get the Lurpy pages," Sloan said, wondering how a man could tell a woman to "come and get" him and court her at the same time. Thank God he'd come to his senses and retrieved his ultimatum. Pillow-hugging really wasn't for him.

Melanie paused, then said, "Thanks for the roses, and the tip about Butterman's Heart Valve."

"Thanks for the apple dumplings." Sloan wanted to lift her into his arms, close his office door and show her how much he needed her. Melanie had yet to come to him; he'd done all the running. Her stare was wary, questioning before she turned and entered her office.

Sloan frowned, picking up a fortune cookie and snapping it open. His claim on Melanie was tenuous at best. *All things are not certain,* it read.

That night, they stood side by side on the elevator. Sloan inhaled Melanie's flowery scent. The image of her soft and clinging in his arms swirled around him. Her rapid sighs echoed in the crowded chamber....

His eyes widened as a small hand explored his backside, moving down his thighs, then between them.

Melanie stared straight ahead, her hand slipping higher and molding his backside. Sloan shifted his weight uncomfortably, unsettled by the stark desire racing through him. She looked up at him, straightened her pin and smiled sweetly before moving off into the crowd. For a moment, Sloan leaned against the wall, trying to place his sweet little wifey-to-be with the confident, professional female moving through the quitting-time crowd.

The November wind caught her hair, the sunlight shimmering through the blond curls. There was a definite sway to Melanie's curved hips, a confidence that nagged at Sloan.

That night, Itty expertly flipped a pancake onto the platter held by his butler. "I like this family stuff. Sort of grows on you—cooking supper while the little woman and the family play pool, you know?''

A round of laughter shot up from the poolroom, and the hard lines of Itty's face changed to a delighted expression. ''Nice of Peaches and Delilah to teach the kid how to play pool, huh? I had her a special cue made and a couple benches made so she can stand up high enough to shoot.''

Sloan traced Melanie's round hips beneath her tight jeans and frowned. Melanie Sue was up to no good; he could feel her moving, shifting around in their uneasy relationship. Then there was Landis circling Melanie's new image....

''I asked Mel to move in with me after Danielle leaves.''

Itty lowered his thick brows and flipped another pancake. ''You watch it, bub. Peaches is the marrying kind.''

''We're doing that, all in good time. We haven't passed the courting stage yet. We haven't had one date.''

''Why not?'' Itty shot back as he stirred the blueberry syrup that was warming in a chafing dish.

''Things are moving rather quickly, Itty—''

''Man, there are priorities and then there is stuff that comes first. You'd better start making lists if you can't figure that out,'' Itty stated flatly.

Later, while Delilah and Itty demonstrated a jitterbug step in which the burly ex-con expertly slung the small, laughing woman around his body, Sloan studied ''Peaches.''

Cuddling Danielle on her lap, she looked innocent enough. There was just something about the pieces that didn't fit....

Melanie glanced up to see Sloan studying her. She looked away quickly, bending to listen to Danielle.

Sloan frowned. Something was definitely amiss in his courtship of M. S. Inganforde. He decided to pick the time and the place for a proper showdown.

Itty, Danielle and Delilah retired to play blackjack, and the old-time jukebox placed a slow dance record beneath the needle. Melanie asked softly, "Would you like to dance, Sloan?"

Snuggling in his arms, she was everything he wanted—a soft, flowery-scented life-mate. They swayed pleasantly, dreamily to the music, Melanie's head tucked safely beneath his chin. For a moment Sloan allowed himself to remember her shy, tentative caresses, the four-poster bed gently creaking—

"I'm not moving in with you, Sloan," Melanie whispered softly against his chest. "Our life-styles are too different.... Our affair—relationship—will do just as well if we live separately."

Sloan tensed and stopped in midsway. For an instant he visualized a lifetime of pillow-hugging, then he reacted instinctively. "Sloan...what are you doing?" Melanie demanded sharply as he picked her up in his arms and carried her into the poolroom.

He plopped her on the pool table, anchoring her by placing his hands on either side of her hips. "What's the deal?" he demanded carefully. "We're in love.... What's the big deal, Mel?"

She shimmered in her mood, obviously struggling to hold her temper. Running a small hand through her curls, Melanie licked her lips slowly, distracting Sloan immediately. He followed the slow, sensuous movement of her tongue with a hunger that startled him.

After clearing her throat, Melanie picked up the two ball and the eight ball. She played with them while Sloan waited for her to speak. He nuzzled the sweet spot behind her ear and she shivered appropriately. "I love you, Mel. Got it?"

One small but firm hand rose to his chest. "Sloan, wait. You've got to give me a chance to work through this, step by step...."

He nibbled on her earlobe, flicking it with his tongue. "Uh-huh. Lay it on me, Mel."

Melanie carefully removed his hand from her soft hips. She leaned back as he studied her closely. "Ah...would you mind stepping back just a little, Sloan? I'm having difficulty breathing...and thinking."

Sloan wasn't reacting well, Melanie thought wildly as he leaned back and crossed his arms over his chest. His stance bore all the earmarks of a frustrated, angry male thwarted in his master plan. She examined the muscle moving rhythmically in his set jaw. If she didn't explain carefully, his delicate ego could be shattered. "This has all happened rather quickly, Sloan. I'm a planner, you know...and our relationship just sort of popped up."

"Damn right, it did. You listened to me spill my guts about the woman I loved and didn't say a word— *We are not having an affair, damn it!*"

She held up her hand and Sloan glared at her, then ran his fingers through his hair. She ached to smooth his mussed, peaked hair. She played with the pool balls and caught Sloan scowling at her slender, white hands.

"Would you mind not doing that?" he asked in a low roar. "Now what is the Major Problem?"

"Darling, please be patient...."

Sloan shook his head, running his hand around his jaw. "What are we doing now, Mel? Setting terms? Making lists? What?" Then he reached for her.

Desperately fighting for space in which to think, Melanie rose to her feet. She frowned and pointed a finger at him. "Stop right there, Raventhrall. Stop calling *all* the moves.... You wanted me to come and get you—"

"Come...down...from...there," Sloan bellowed, moving around the table like a hunter circling his trapped prey.

Melanie tossed him the eight ball. She couldn't remember him acting so pushy with his bodacious amazons. A small trickle of fear rippled through her as he moved toward her as though he planned to carry her off to his lair. "Oh dear, I knew you'd be upset. You're not taking this well at all."

Sloan shot the ball into the side pocket without looking. It rattled noisily with the force of his roll. He took a deep breath and said between his teeth, "You've been making lists, haven't you? What happened to the pros and cons of our relationship, Mel? Let me know what you decided. As the other half of our relationship, it would be nice to know."

Melanie tossed him the other ball, which met a similar fate. Sloan braced his hands on the side of the table and glared up at her. "You've got that look, Mel. As though you've put together a suitable, compromisable, profitable package . . . and damn it, you're driving me up the wall."

"You can't have it all your way, Sloan," Melanie insisted, realizing that if she couldn't hold her own with him, she would always feel cheated.

His eyebrows shot up. "My way? What the hell is My Way?"

She held up one finger. "You do the courting." Then she held up a second finger. "I move in with you. The typical male-dominated relationship. You may be the star player at Standards, Sloan. But I want equal billing in our relationship."

"That's the package, Mel. Always has been." Sloan took a deep breath. "I'm the man . . . I set the pace."

"Until now," she stated firmly. "You wanted me to come and get you. I intend to do just that." He nodded slowly as if just realizing how serious she was and the implications of his demand. "You're a dominating, dynamic man, Sloan Raventhrall," she began carefully. "But if I let you run with the ball now, I'll never be able to hold my own with you."

"The hell you say," he returned angrily. "Tell me more."

Struggling to clarify her emotions before an unsympathetic ruffled male ego, Melanie eased down from the pool table and primly straightened her sweater over her jeans.

"It's just like picking me up and charging in here, Sloan. You've got to admit that doesn't do a lot for a woman's dignity. *Everything has been on your terms.*"

After a long moment, Sloan shook his head. "Women," he stated as if her sex explained everything.

Then he walked away.

"Women," Sloan repeated two nights later as he worked out at the gym. His body ached, taut with the need to take M. S. Inganforde every time her flowery scent swirled around him.

He bent to increase the pressure on the rowing machine, then paused as Melanie's scent drifted around him. He looked up to see her dressed in a red-hot leotard and warm-up stockings. Her creamy, soft thighs shimmered in the fluorescent lights. The body suit hugged and emphasized every delectable inch of her curves. A sensual need ripped through Sloan, and because she'd penetrated his lair, his private thinking area, he snarled, "What are you doing here, Mel? You never work out."

She smiled sweetly, smoothing his hair. Then, bending down, she kissed his mouth slowly. When her lips lifted, Sloan shook his head to clear it. When his eyes focused, they flowed over Melanie's delicious attributes. "Don't look so upset, Raventhrall. This gym is for everyone. Danielle and mother are on the bicycles. Itty is doing the laundry. He's thinking of investing in a new company that promises an environmental laundry soap."

Scooting into the rowing machine next to him, Melanie adjusted the stirrups to her feet and started pulling the oars, flexing her limbs against the machine's tension.

Sloan stared at the sensuous, rippling, strong beckoning of her body. With little effort he visualized her in the four-poster, those pale soft thighs flexing rhythmically... "You'll hurt yourself," he muttered darkly, trying to put the image out of his mind. A muscular Adonis stopped moentarily to stare at Melanie, then moved off slowly after loan glared at him. To keep himself from grabbing her and unning to the nearest shower stall, Sloan began to row lowly. The image of his nymph and the career woman orking until a droplet of sweat trickled down the shimery crevice of her breasts and startled him.

He rowed furiously, trying to work out his temper. Sweet, uddly, delectable life-mates nestled in their silky bowers aiting for their lovers amid a bed of rose petals. M. S. Inanforde—career woman—worked out until she sweated.

Sloan glanced at the damp area between her breasts, noting the rippling flow. Desire stark and primitive shot rough him, nothing like the sweet, wooing sensation his ymph caused.

Staring at her body, Sloan did not doubt that Mel could meet his sensual demands . . . that her hunger would match is own. The thought unsettled him.

Melanie kept pace with him, their movements matching moothly. "Don't be so upset, Raventhrall," she said after few moments. "You're acting like your ego has been amaged."

Sloan speeded up the pace, and Melanie matched him. He oted the soft flow of feminine flesh swelling over the top f the low costume. "You're really weird, Inganforde," he aid between breaths.

"Hey. What can I say? I'm a woman."

"Uh-huh," he answered tightly, remembering her responses to him. Other women had chased him to his satisaction, but ladyloves just didn't . . . turn the tables. It wasn't a the romantic handbook. He shook a drop of sweat from is forehead and noted the damp sheen to Melanie's face nd chest. How he longed to kiss the deep valley of those oft, sweet, fragrant breasts . . . to tell her of his love.

"I want an equal relationship, Sloan," Melanie said, ming her breathing to the machine. "It's just that you've ot some pretty old-fashioned ideas about women—"

"For instance?" Sloan ignored the sweat running down his body and fought his anger. He watched the muscles flex in her soft thighs. Somehow he hadn't realized how strong his ladylove was.

"You act like I'm a corporate takeover, Sloan. You've already got the merger planned. When do I do my part?"

He stared at her blankly and blew a drop of sweat from his upper lip. "What the hell are you raving about now, Inganforde?"

She smiled smugly. "Equal opportunity, my friend. You wanted me to come get you and I like the idea. I've never practiced wooing a lover and want to do my part in this affair."

"Affair?" Sloan closed his eyes and wondered where his sweet, shy ladylove had hidden herself. He summed up his feelings about her proposal in one word—"Dumb."

Melanie arched an eyebrow at him and winked. "But fun. Come on, Raventhrall. Don't be such a stick-in-the-mud. Go with the flow. Try something new."

"Such as?"

"I've never had to court a man, Raventhrall. You presented the idea, and I find it to be fascinating . . . after all, if things work out this could be my last chance to try my skills. You wouldn't want me wondering about it later, would you?"

Three days later, Jessica Villiancourt stared at her brother. "Sloan, what has happened to you? You never used to let affairs with women get you down. You look like a brooding old lion, hiding out in his den."

Sloan shifted Danielle to his shoulders and ignored her pleas to giddy-up. "This isn't an affair. And Inganforde is *very* different. We . . . are . . . not—repeat, *not*—having an affair. She's the woman I intend to marry."

Jessica hooted as Danielle leapt into her arms. "I knew it would happen to your uncle, Danielle. It was just a matter of time. Tell me about this Inganforde, Danny."

Danielle kissed her mother's cheek and hugged her. "I missed you. But Melanie was neat. She's like Sleeping Beauty, awakened by the prince's kiss. I saw Sloan kiss her once, and Melanie blinked after that, just like she was waking up. Her face got all pink and she stuttered."

Her mother sat and held her on her lap. "And what happened to Uncle Sloan?"

"Oh, he got all dreamy-looking. Sort of hungry-looking, too. After that, he must have had a bad dream, 'cause he moaned all night. He squashes his pillow when he sleeps...." Jessica's giggle rippled through the air.

"Lay off the kid, Jessie," Sloan rumbled, foraging for a place to hide. He settled for sprawling at the other end of his couch and flipping through a magazine, while his sister grinned. A stuffed monkey tumbled onto his lap and beamed up at him with button eyes. "Lay off," he muttered, allowing the toy to cling to him with hairy arms.

"He's in love, Danny. Women always spoil him, and this one isn't playing the game, is she, Sloan? She isn't letting you call the shots. You're probably trying to tie her up in a neat little bundle, ignoring the possibility that she's a contemporary career woman with her own way of doing things."

Sloan stared at her blankly, then scowled. "Women!"

Jessica's giggle rippled over him, raising the hair on the back of his neck. "When do I get to meet her? Is she long and lanky with tremendous—"

"Mel is short and mean. I work with her. She's mixed up about our roles," Sloan snapped. "That's about the sum of it."

"Uh-huh," Jessica said without conviction. "I still want to meet her."

   That evening Jessica, Danielle, Delilah and Melanie sat
at Itty's long dining room table with Sloan. Itty and the
butler swished into the huge, chandelier-lighted room, carrying trays of food. "Chow. Real grub," Itty explained,
unloading mashed potatoes, gravy, roast turkey and cran-
berry sauce. "Since Delilah and me are headed for Las Vegas over Thanksgiving, I thought now would be a good time
for the family dinner."

   "How nice," Jessica said, smirking at Sloan. "Since
Danielle will be going home with me, that leaves poor Sloan
out on his own...just like an orphan."

   "I'll make do."

   "I have plans for Sloan," Melanie said in her husky, firm
voice as her hand moved across his knee. Sloan jumped
when her fingers squeezed his thigh gently. He almost
blushed.

   "Oh, my," Jessica exclaimed when she stopped giggling.

   After dinner, the women retreated to the poolroom, and
Itty and Sloan shared a glass of good bourbon while they
debated the female mind.

   "It's the only way. I'm getting my sugarplum drunk in
Las Vegas. We'll get married before she can back out. Seems
fair enough to me," Itty rumbled around the lollipop that
he sucked in lieu of smoking his cigar. He downed a good
measure of bourbon. "What's your plan, boy? Better be
good, 'cause Peaches is a sweet little thing."

   "She makes lists," Sloan muttered darkly, watching her
line up for a difficult shot.

   "Plays a great game of poker. Just like her mother. Sweet
little things, the pair of them."

   Danielle tugged on his leg and Sloan bent to lift her up for
a hug. She ran her small hand around his jaw and rubbed
her nose against his. "Are you gonna marry Melanie, Uncle Sloan? And am I going to have my cousins out of you,
like my mama says?"

   Itty snickered around his lollipop.

Later Melanie and Danielle sat on the floor, playing a last round of jacks. They spoke intimately, pausing in the middle of tossing the ball to discuss something intently, throwing stealthy glances at Sloan.

Melanie blushed and fidgeted with her hair as Danielle grinned widely. When Danielle climbed up on Sloan's lap, she kissed his lips with a loud smack. "Melanie thinks you're cute, Uncle Sloan. But she says you are really old-fashioned and not..." She struggled for the word, and then her eyes lighted. "You are not sys-system—atic, and it drives her nuts."

That night, Melanie's apartment buzzer sounded. She smiled gently as the buzzer rang again, jabbed by an impatient, angry caller. "Yes?" she answered sweetly. "Who is it?"

"Lay off, Mel. It's cold out here."

"Raventhrall?"

Within minutes, Sloan stood in front of her apartment door, looming over her. He smiled nastily, his hand braced against the doorframe. "Are you going to invite me in, or are the neighbors in for a surprise? They've probably never seen an old-fashioned man make a scene."

"You're unhappy. Please come in," she returned, pleased that his gaze had swung down her body. The black teddy and matching peignoir had just the right effect on him. Sloan did wonderful things for her ego.

In the next moment, he discarded his coat over her sofa, loosened his tie and unbuttoned his shirt. "Make yourself at home," Melanie offered with a tender smile, taking his coat to hang up in her closet.

Sloan kicked off his shoes and stood there in his unmatched socks, looking wary, ruffled and appealing. His appearance begged for a soothing hand, though his scowl left little welcome.

"Would you like a piece of apple pie, Sloan?"

"I want you and you know it," he said roughly, walking toward her. In the next instant, he carried her into her bedroom and kicked the door shut.

Melanie landed in a heap of black lace in the center of her four-poster bed. When aroused, Sloan played a very good Rhett, she decided as he came down beside her, shaking the bed.

Through the shadows, his face loomed over her, his head braced on one hand. With the other hand, he toyed with the ribbons of her teddy. He tugged one bow open, studying the curve of soft, pale flesh.

Because she knew that Sloan weighed the problem before him and because he looked so alone, Melanie placed her hand on his hard chest and ventured softly, "I missed you, darling."

"Uh-huh." Sloan looked very vulnerable as he tugged open another bow. "You know, I'm not exactly happy with this situation, Mel."

"Oh...poor baby," Melanie soothed, rummaging through the hairs on his chest to find his nipple. She bent to gently kiss it, then the other. When she looked up, Sloan had closed his eyes, breathing unevenly.

"You're tough, Inganforde," he whispered rawly, running his hand across the lace covering her hip.

Spreading herself over Sloan's hard body, Melanie stretched luxuriously and nuzzled his hard, stubble-covered jaw. Sloan was so sturdy, unbreakable. She caressed his taut throat and kissed the base of it, listening to his rapid heartbeat. The traditional male, Sloan needed to be taken into the mode of modern-day courtship a step at a time, she decided. For now, all that was important was the slightly rough, tender way he tore the ribbons apart, drawing her breasts against his chest with the air of a man who had hungered and was now on the brink of being satisfied.

Melanie stretched and molded her body to his hard, aroused one. She delighted in his expression, one of stark hunger, one of tenderness and love...as if she were the only woman on earth.

"Time out," she whispered, referring to the matter of clearing up their respective roles. She bent to brush her lips over his. "Love me, darling."

Ten

"Raventhrall... Inganforde... back off," Justin Devereau ordered sharply from the head of the conference table a week later. "We're a team here at Standards, remember? Grandma's Nutty Cookies is a small business with a sweet little old lady who wants to open up her company to stockholders. Stockholm Motors is a major company set to merge with another with a strong CEO. We're balancing ideas here, not starting a war." He glanced at Sloan who was standing and glaring down at Melanie. Several inches lower than the star player's face, she returned his scowl. The remainder of the men at the conference table doodled in their leather notebooks and waited for the third confrontation of the day to glide over their heads.

Devereau cleared his throat and glanced at his wristwatch. "Ah...let's take a ten minute break. Sloan, you and M.S. see me in my office, okay?"

"After you, Mel," Sloan offered as Devereau exited the room.

"After you, star player," Melanie purred.

In the chairman's office, they sat in front of his desk. "You two have a problem," Devereau said. "I want it solved before we lose any more time debating minor issues. Grandma's has growth potential, but it's a new company with a few setbacks. Sloan, you're putting confidence in an elderly woman who rules that company with an iron hand. Chivalry is great, but not in stocks and bonds. Maybe M.S. is right, Stockholm Motors looks more worthy of our investor's portfolios. It's a small point, not big enough to mention, considering the market is up and trading is good."

Devereau sat back, created a temple with his fingertips and asked softly, "Could something else be at the bottom of this squabbling?"

Sloan sat back, his jaw set and a muscle ticking ominously across it. "Ask Ms. Power-monger here."

"M.S.? Is there a personal problem I should know about? I've noticed you've changed your style and you're attracting several strong customers. Maybe the tension is getting to you...."

Melanie smoothed her business pin and straightened the soft vee-shaped collar of her blouse. She crossed her legs and studied the neat crease of her slacks. "Sloan isn't coping. He's nervous and grouchy."

Devereau swung to Sloan. "Problems?"

"Her," Sloan snapped. "She's getting on my nerves."

"Really?" Devereau asked with interest. "Causing you problems?"

"She makes lists...."

"We're trying to work things out, Mr. Devereau," Melanie interrupted. "You're right, we do have a small problem. But I can assure you that it will work out. Could we discuss the matter in private?" she asked. "I'm certain we can reach a compromise."

After Devereau left the room, Sloan muttered, "Compromise, my—"

"Move in with me, Sloan," Melanie asked softly, slipping onto his lap.

Sloan laid his weary head on her shoulder and nuzzled the vee of her blouse until it opened for his lips. She noted the dark circles beneath his lashes and kissed them lightly. "I asked you first."

She stroked his head gently, arching momentarily as his lips trailed down to nibble at her breast. "Ah . . . Sloan, would you like to stay home and putter around?"

"Putter?" he asked with interest, adjusting her thighs across his hardening body.

"Oh, play poker, have El Lobo and a few people over—"

"At my place?" he asked hopefully, inhaling the fresh, flowery scent swirling around her strawberry birthmark and ignoring the businesswoman's crisp perfume clinging to her clothes.

"We're still in the first stages of developing our relationship, honey," she whispered, nibbling on his ear and noting with satisfaction that his breathing had changed into an uneven pattern.

Beneath her, Sloan's large body tensed. "Stages?" he asked cautiously.

"Mmm. You know, putting together a system that suits us both. Being practical about giving and taking. Doing things together. . . ." She nuzzled the intimate scent of soap and man clinging to his throat.

Sloan's hands eased her slightly away. "What gives, Inganforde? Are you making lists?"

Melanie tensed at his cautious tone. She hoped the folded list in her jacket pocket would not rustle. "Sloan, you must know that our relationship—our different life-styles and personalities—call for clear thinking—"

She almost fell off his lap as he stood up. His jaw tensed, the muscle working steadily as he looked at her for a long

moment. His eyes darkened with sadness, then it was gone.
"You are hopeless, Mel," he said quietly before leaving.

Two days later, Melanie snapped her pencil, discarded the
two parts and adjusted her lapel pin. If Sloan wanted romance, he should have it.

She'd never attempted to snare a life-mate, but if Sloan
needed seduction, kisses and romance, he'd have it on a
platter. She flipped open her personal notebook and jotted
down several notes, then, keying into the company computer, she sent a message to Sloan. *Hi honey. Dinner?
Dancing? M.S.*

Within seconds, a message arrived on her screen. *When?
Where?*

Your choice.

Who pays? Sloan asked.

Me? Dutch? she returned, suggesting that each pay their
own.

No deal. Men pay. Code of the West.

Melanie fought the slight anger riffling through her. She
was determined to prove to Sloan that she could be seductive, romantic and a professional, contemporary woman.
She snapped Mrs. Lacey's file shut and slid it into her file
drawer. Seconds later, she entered Sloan's office. Rumpled
fortune cookie wrappers sprawled across his desk, the thin
strips of fortune neatly placed in rows.

"What's the problem, Mel?" Sloan asked, sweeping the
wrappers into his trash can with his left foot. His right one
didn't move from his desk.

Melanie picked up the wrapper that had fallen to the carpeting and tossed it into the trash can. "'Code of the West'?
I'm not happy with you, Sloan."

"Give me a break, Inganforde. There are things that nag
a man's ego, and being placed on lists is one of them."

Melanie took a deep breath. "At the moment, you're n
exactly making me happy. This is my first affair or re
tionship...whatever. *I want to be a participant.*"

In the next instant, Sloan's feet hit the carpeting. Then
was on his feet, advancing toward her with a look of dete
mined sensuality. He snagged her wrist gently, drew her t
ward him and encircled her with his arms, lifting he
Against her lips, Sloan ordered softly, "Don't...don't ev
put me on your lists like an account, Mel. Romance isn't
clinical affair—a well-organized portfolio."

Melanie blinked, noting the tense muscles holding he
Sloan was very, very angry. "I know that.... What do y
propose?" she managed unevenly, testing his strength as s
tried to draw away. Sloan's jaw tensed and his fingers
mained, shackling her without pain.

His mouth moved slowly, seductively, warmly across her
parting it gently. "I want..." he whispered rawly as
hands cupped her buttocks and squeezed gently. "I wa
you to move in with me."

"Sloan..." Melanie's throat tightened at Sloan's da
gerous, challenging expression.

He nibbled on her earlobe, and Melanie squirmed une
ily as warmth flooded her lower limbs. "I don't think we'
ready just yet...." she breathed as Sloan's hand slid b
neath her legs and eased gently upward.

"Live dangerously, Inganforde," he murmured agai
her ear. "Dinner...dancing...on me. I'll pick you up
eight."

"Ah...Sloan, I'm picking up Mother and Itty at t
airport. Then we're working on another Thanksgiving di
ner...."

Against her throat, Sloan cursed softly.

Itty basted the Thanksgiving turkey, then leaned agai
the counter, sipping a small glass of root beer. "Me
secretly married...just like a kid. Delilah wants to

Peaches alone. Ah, life's great, ain't it? Who would think that a guy like me could snag a classy act like Delilah?''

The beefy ex-con leveled a penetrating stare at Sloan, who was tearing lettuce for a green salad. "You ain't been putting the moves on my sweet little stepdaughter, have you, S.R.? Delilah wants to plan a big wedding for Melanie, long white gown and everything. I'm planning a four-tier cake and a big bash. I've always wanted to try an ice sculpture for the punch bowl—maybe a giant baseball mitt.''

Sloan traced the rounded curves of Melanie's derriere as she bent over the pool table, sighting up the three ball for the corner pocket. His relationship with Melanie was not secure; he wanted her committed to a lifetime of romance. "Inganforde is not the white-gown-and-wedding-cake type," he muttered, irritated that Melanie had included him on her lists. "She'd probably carry a notebook and a checklist to the altar.''

"'Course she's the bride type," Itty returned as he tested the boiling potatoes with a fork. "She's sweet and dainty, just like her mother, and I don't want her driving all over Kansas City at night by herself. You follow her home tonight and see that she gets in her place, or I will—" He paused, looked sharply at Sloan and frowned thoughtfully before replacing the lid on the pot. "My little girl had better not be compromised, S.R.... You know—unmarried and in a family way. My grandkids—''

Melanie squealed, tossed her pool cue onto the table and hugged her mother who beamed.

"Delilah told her," Itty murmured, grinning as Melanie ran toward the kitchen.

She hugged Itty, congratulating him, and in the next instant launched herself at Sloan and began crying. Tucking her beneath his chin and wrapping his arms around her protectively, Sloan looked helplessly at Itty.

"Women," Itty murmured, grinning and tugging a tear
ful Delilah against his side. "Ain't they great?"

Monday morning, Sloan idly tossed wadded pape
through the miniature hoop into his trash can. Melanie ha
taken the news well about her mother's marriage, chirpin
happily throughout the magnificent dinner Itty had pre
pared. Then she had escaped to her apartment without
backward glance at Sloan. He'd given her the weekend t
adjust to the new circumstances. He wanted Melanie in sta
ble mental condition before resuming his pursuit.

The word "affair" was unappealing when referring t
Melanie. Farm life in Iowa seemed far away. He sighe
wistfully, remembering the creamy warmth of her bod
curled to him in the big, soft four-poster bed. Winter nigh
stretched before him, long and cold and boring.

He crumpled another paper and tossed it through th
hoop. Melanie was a shifty commodity, her career imag
acting as a veneer for the tempting, delightful nymph withir
Sloan automatically clicked on his computer, checkin
messages on the screen. Pork bellies were down... Amalga
mated Juices rising sharply... Jennifer in accounting ha
produced a six-pound girl named Emily... M. S. Ingan
forde had moved into number-six suite, recently vacated b
Dave Moore, please route all mail to her there....

A larger office, Melanie's new suite contained a wash
room and a couch, exactly the status that would make M. S
Inganforde happy. He jerked open his fortune cooki
wrapper and read, *Good things come in small packages. B
patient.*

That night, Melanie's delicious body bumped gently int
his in the crowded elevator. A delicate pat found his lef
buttocks, then swatted his right. Sloan tried to ignore hi
body's immediate response. He looked down at her waril
and found her shooting him up a seductive look beneath he

lashes. "Dinner?" she whispered, edging fractionally closer. She stood on tiptoe to whisper again, "Me?"

"Celebrating your new office, Mel-dear? High on power?" he answered quietly, aware that her small hand was gently prowling his backside.

"Mmm. How about it? I'll pick you up at eight," she asked just as Jonsey in public relations glanced curiously at them.

Sloan gritted his teeth. "I could pick you up. That's standard for a date."

Her laughter rippled through the elevator, and people stared at Sloan. "You're delicious, Sloan . . . absolutely fascinating as an endangered species."

"Lay off," he muttered, aware that his cheeks were warming as Georgette smothered a knowing smile.

After another low, feminine laugh, Melanie stood on tiptoe to kiss his cheek. "You're sweet, Sloan."

"Sweet," he repeated through his teeth. "Is that how you see me?"

She patted his bottom. "Terribly sweet and old-fashioned. The traditional male."

Sloan snagged her prowling hand and locked his hand around her wrist. The rest of the people in the elevator moved into the lobby, momentarily leaving them alone. He smiled tightly. "Just the perfect material for an affair, eh, Inganforde?" he asked quietly, dangerously.

"Perfect," she returned blithely, straightening his tie. Sloan had the flashing mental image of Melanie checking off number one on her list.

"When are you making your move, Mel?" he asked, watching her eyes widen and her lips part with surprise.

She lowered her lashes, clearly caught in the act of an outrageous deed. She blushed, and Sloan found himself fascinated by the play of assertive career woman versus seductive nymph. "Well . . . tonight . . . if all goes well," she admitted softly. "I have big plans."

"Dinner? Dancing? Seduction?" he asked in rapid order as her pulse began to pound beneath his fingertips. "Then maybe ask me away for a quiet weekend at the lake. The Love Tide Resort is standard for a lovers' weekend."

She adjusted her professional pin, trying to shield her blush from him. Nestled in the Ozark hills of Missouri, the secluded resort was a lovers' delight. "It's a cozy, little cabin overlooking the lake. Has a fireplace."

"A perfect weekend rendezvous?" he asked softly, feeling his anger rise. He wanted commitments for a lifetime, not playtime. Clearly Melanie needed refreshing on the theory of life-mates. "I'll want a list of your plan, Mel. Spell out the formalities and just exactly what you expect from me."

"Sloan, you're being difficult."

"I'm a traditional male . . . an endangered species. . . . I'll walk you to your car. . . . I'll pick you up at eight. That's the standard procedure for a date."

"Oh, you're hurt," she whispered soothingly, moving closer to him. She stroked his jaw, nibbling at it until Sloan relented and allowed her to trail small, soft kisses across his lips.

"You know I don't like surprises," Melanie stated firmly from her corner of Sloan's black beast. The headlights swung onto the Love Tide's welcoming sign, and the winter wind slashed a spray of dried oak leaves across the windshield. Freezing rain battered the exterior of the cab. "I canceled the reservation because of the bad weather."

"Lovers' rendezvous are not canceled like ball games, Melanie Sue," Sloan returned, parking the vehicle in front of number-seven cabin. The rock-hewn cabin looked cold and forbidding. "You've got to be flexible in the sweetheart business."

"I should work on Mother's and Itty's reception for next Saturday," Melanie returned stubbornly. Sloan acted quickly, once he'd set his priorities. It seemed she was at the top of his list. Playing an intuitive game against her step-by-step campaign, Sloan threatened her assertive plans for equal opportunity. "There is an immense amount of work to be done for a proper reception ... caterers, a dance band specializing in jitterbug music.... One has to plan in advance—those bands are difficult to secure at a moment's notice."

Sloan turned off the lights and toyed with the curls at the back of her neck. "Give it a rest, Mel."

She swatted his prowling fingers aside. "Just what will we do for the entire weekend?"

"Get to know each other without interference," he stated firmly, opening her door. The movement brought his arm across her breasts and she inhaled sharply. Sloan's eyes darkened as he glanced down at her. "I've missed you, honey," he whispered, allowing his arm to press gently across her full breasts.

Melanie inhaled sharply and glanced down Sloan's lean body. Dressed in a heavy sweater and worn jeans, his hair mussed by the wind—and the many times he'd raked his fingers through it—Sloan looked tempting. She visualized snuggling close to him, kissing and hugging and rubbing his hairy calf with her foot. She blushed as he continued looking at her intently. "Ah, Sloan...I didn't mean to attack you that night after our date. I'm sorry I ripped the pocket on your shirt."

"Pockets were meant to be ripped," he offered gallantly.

She looked down at her tightly laced fingers, remembering how tightly she had held Sloan—desperately, feverishly. "I'm nervous."

Sloan nuzzled her hot cheek. "Exciting, isn't it?"

She looked at him helplessly, feeling desperately uncomfortable. "Sloan, I've never done this before.... Do you think we could go someplace and have dinner first?"

"We picked up the groceries on the way, honey. Everything on your lists," he said patiently. "Come on."

Since he had been patient through her organized search of the tiny grocery store, she relented. Not every man or woman would wait while she restacked a display of sardines. Sloan had offered tips on the artistry of can-balancing, and in her nervous state, Melanie had upset a pyramid of oranges.

Inside the cabin, Melanie clutched her coat while Sloan placed the groceries in the tiny kitchenette and started the fire. Their two overnight bags sat on the immense four-poster bed, a sign of intimacy that unsettled her. Her paisley print bag looked very feminine against Sloan's black leather case. Sloan's tall body, crouched before the fireplace, seemed to take up more than its share of the small cabin.

The flames outlined his hard features, the stark power of his unshaven jaw. She shivered suddenly. Sloan wanted a commitment from her.

"I've never done this before," she said again softly, aching to have him hold her.

He blew on the tiny flames, urging them into life gently, just as he'd kissed her into that savage hunger on their date. "Neither have I."

"You haven't?"

"No one else was worth leaving the comfort of my home and hearth." Sloan's expression slid into slight irritation. "You seem to have the idea that my past is littered with sleazy affairs or, at best, one-nighters. It isn't, and it won't be."

The bodacious amazons hovered around Melanie, taunting her. "What about your wife?"

He shifted warily, prodding the flames with a stick. "A perfect corporate wife. At ease at parties, understanding when I came home late. Totally efficient . . . a woman who didn't need me in her life."

Because he seemed so vulnerable, Melanie murmured, "I need you."

Sloan returned the tender admission slowly. "I know. Just as I need you. That's why we're an even match."

"It's dark early now," she whispered, as he turned to stare at her intently. Sloan rose slowly, stretched and yawned, and shot her a sensuous, hungry look. "Sloan, this could be a disaster," she managed as he padded to her.

"Sweetheart. Honey.... Leave the worrying to me." Sloan gently stripped her coat from her and tossed it onto a cozy chair. "We're here because we're exploring—"

"What will we do all weekend?" she managed in a squeak and wondered how many more ways they could explore. Rick had allowed her to set the pace, to push and prod and temize. Sloan was another matter. As a basic, pin-striped career woman, she hadn't examined the delicacies of the perfect touch at an exact moment. She shivered as she remembered the way Sloan had levered her gently over his body, his fingers exploring her exquisitely....

He gently raked her curls back from her forehead, framing her face with large, safe hands. "We'll take things as they come. First we put the groceries away and start supper. Then we lounge before the fire, maybe play a game or two of poker, or work on your lists for the reception. Then there's the marshmallows to roast—"

She stepped closer, drawn by the warm security of his body in her unsettled seas. "What about unpacking? When do we do that? Sloan, are you certain you haven't ever done this before?"

"Not once." He bent to pick her up and carried her to the overstuffed armchair, settling down to cradle her on his lap. The flames blazed, crackling and filling the room with warmth.

"This is going too quickly," Melanie whispered uneven-

ly against his chest. She needed to work on her methods o
operation, her lists.... Instead she clung to Sloan's muscu
lar shoulders as a lifeline.

"Not quickly enough," he muttered over her head
stroking the rounded line of her hip. He squeezed gently. "
want to go to bed with you each night, and wake up witl
you each morning. I'm not geared for affairs. This one i
bad on my nerves. I missed a merger the other day tha
could have cost a prime account."

"It's living together," she whispered, feeling tears burr
her lids. "We're just not a matched set.... You'd be a dis
aster as a life-mate. You squeeze the toothpaste tube in th
middle while I roll it from the bottom."

"We're a perfect match," he returned gently.

"We fight. Devereau will notice."

"Lay off, Inganforde," Sloan rasped heavily, shifting he
slightly over his lap. Aroused and waiting, his body tense
around her. She snuggled to the hard comfort, savoring th
way he groaned uncomfortably. It was wonderful to knov
that she could affect Sloan with such intensity. She wrig
gled again experimenting with the tense muscles beneath her
and Sloan breathed unevenly. In a gust of self-confidence
Melanie looped her arms around his neck and tugged hin
closer for her kiss.

Sloan reacted wonderfully, hungrily parting his mouth t
hers, taking and giving and searching....

She slipped her hands beneath his sweater to find hard
warm flesh and muscle. Kneading his chest with her finger
tips, Melanie gave herself to Sloan's seeking, hungry kiss.

An hour later, Melanie stared at the melting ice cream an
the puddle on the kitchen's tile floor. "I just don't under
stand any of this," she muttered, clutching Sloan's shir
around her pleasantly warm and sated body.

Sloan, naked and wonderful, bent to clean the puddle. H
moved around the tiny alcove, placing groceries into the re
frigerator. She traced the long, taut line of his back, th

long, powerful legs. His shoulders bore red marks and, reminded of her passion, Melanie blushed. He'd barely secured protection when she'd spread him out on the bed like a tray of delicious hors d'oeuvres. "What are we going to do, Sloan?" she asked for the fifth time.

"Put the groceries away, honey." Sloan bent to kiss her tender, swollen lips.

"But it's all so silly—the groceries should have been put away before...before..." she floundered helplessly as Sloan patted her bottom.

"Emergencies arise, my love. Don't look so shattered."

She glanced at the mussed bed, the clothing scattered around the room, and remembered everything, clearly. She blushed as Sloan bent to kiss the spot behind her ear. "I don't understand any of this," she repeated.

She'd planned a romantic evening, a candlelight dinner and the chance to model her stunning new lace nightwear. Humming softly, Sloan opened a bottle of wine and poured it into glasses. He handed one to her and studied her intently. "You look shocked, Mel. Why don't you take a long bubble bath and I'll fix dinner?"

Once inside the bathroom, Melanie carefully turned the lock. She badly needed the privacy to examine her emotions. Apparently Sloan could ignite her savage hungers with a gentle kiss. The idea startled and alarmed her.

Settling into the fragrant, bubble-filled waters, Melanie inventoried her well-loved body. Sloan treated her with absolute respect, gearing his pace to hers and sending her over the edge with the tiniest pressure low on her body.... She lifted her fire-red-tinted toes and studied the long, slender line of her legs.

A light knock on the door startled her. "Go away. I'm busy."

Sloan entered with a low chuckle, handing another glass of wine to her. He grinned when she edged deeper in the mounds of bubbles. "You're sulking, my love. You planned

my seduction step by step and then shot the whole idea to
smithereens." He settled comfortably against the doorframe and sipped his wine. His unbuttoned jeans sagged low
on his stomach, reminding her of a sexy calendar. Sloan's
rumpled, unshaven, devastating male look would arouse an
eighty-year-old spinster. "Dinner is ready when you are. Or
we could warm it later," he offered in a low, sensuous drawl.

His gaze trailed over the bubbles thoughtfully.

"Later?" she asked in a voice unlike her own. Sloan
placed their glasses aside and lifted her from the tub. Water
dripped to the floor as he held her easily, kissing her gently.
When she could speak, Melanie whispered unevenly,
"Sloan, there is water dripping everywhere. The door was
locked...."

"Locks were meant to be picked. You're cute, Inganforde. Cute and cuddly and lovable. I can't resist you."

She blinked, fighting for reality. Trying to keep her balance, she clung to him. "Why?"

"I love you." His heart beat heavily beneath her palm.

"Your jeans are getting wet," she managed as he held her
closer. Her pale reflection filled his dark, sensuous eyes.

"They'll dry...." Sloan cuddled her closer, opening his
hand to caress her wet thigh. "Would you rather have dinner later?" he asked tenderly.

The next morning, Melanie awoke to the sound of her
stomach growling. Displaced, she struggled out of the tangle
of heavy limbs and tangled quilts. Rain battered the windows of the warm cabin, and Sloan grunted as her elbow
nudged his ribs. Melanie blinked, drawing the quilt up to her
chin. As yet, she hadn't met one of the criteria on her list for
the Seduction of Sloan. She shivered with an ominous chill.
Sloan eased to his side, the bare light glowing on his broad
shoulders.

Her body reacted quickly, frightening her. Trying to sta-
bilize her unsteady emotions, Melanie slipped from the bed
and padded to the fireplace. Feeding another log into the

fire, she huddled beneath the blanket and settled down to gaze into the flames.

Sloan was the picture of a perfect lover—kind, considerate and sturdy beneath her unexplainable savagery.

Melanie shook her head. She wanted equal opportunity in their relationship, meeting him fully. She slid a stealthy glance at the tumbled bed, the clothing scattered in untidy bundles. Their bags lay tossed aside, unused, like her plans.

The bed creaked. "Come to bed, honey," Sloan urged sleepily in the darkness.

"We didn't do the dishes," she muttered blankly, clutching the blanket to her. "I didn't even use a towel after my bath...."

"Are you hungry?" he asked quietly, suddenly crouching beside her. He stroked her cheek with his fingertip.

Her stomach growled on cue, and Melanie stared at him helplessly. A tear she'd been fighting oozed from her lid and clung to her lashes as her vision of Sloan's face blurred. "Oh, Sloan. I don't understand any of this."

Sloan leaned his stubbled cheek against hers gently. "Think of it as balancing Itty's portfolio. There are the good, solid investments bearing long-term yields...."

She looked at him, her hopes rising to understand the emotions racing through her. He kissed her shoulder, nuzzling her throat. "Then think of Itty's quirky investments. They equate to this little jaunt. We're learning about each other, sweetheart. Making the pieces fit."

"Logic seems to be forgotten, Sloan. We're..." She glanced uneasily at the rumpled bed and thought about her carefully planned list lying unused in her discarded, rumpled jeans.

"...in love, my dear heart." Sloan nuzzled her curls and stood slowly to tug his jeans on.

"What are you doing?" she asked as he opened the door and walked out, letting a gust of cold rain blow into the cabin.

A few moments later, Sloan opened the door again and shivered. He hopped on one bare foot, as though he'd stepped on a sharp pebble. The lush bouquet of roses and daisies filling his arms trembled in the half light. Rain glittered on the petals and the ferns when he closed the door. "Oh, darling...." Melanie murmured softly as she stood, allowing the blanket to fall aside.

There in the shadows, Sloan paused, his features tightening. Then he walked toward her. "Do you have any idea how happy you've made me, sweetheart? How beautiful you look with the firelight behind you and your eyes filled with me?" he asked huskily.

Blushing wildly, Melanie accepted the flowers, lowering the bouquet to shield her breasts.

Then Sloan was looming near—warming her, bending to kiss her sweetly.

At dawn Melanie hummed quietly, arranging Sloan's shaving kit next to her toiletries on the cabin's small shelf. She pushed back the sleeves of her seduction peignoir and placed his shampoo next to her scented one, his razor near her feminine pink model. Then she placed his shampoo next to his razor and her shampoo next to her razor, studying the effect. His comb rested against her brush. The variety of her cosmetics did not blend with the separation of their toiletries. Toothbrushes were not made to be placed apart, she decided in a whimsical flurry, rearranging bottles and brushes and toothbrushes.

"Inganforde, what the hell are you doing in there?" Sloan roared from the bed.

"Go back to sleep, darling." Melanie studied the toothbrushes and two tubes of toothpaste—one plain and one mint flavored. She decided to place them all upright in a cup.

Sloan's big hand slapped against the doorframe. Unshaven, looking worn, and his hair rumpled from her fin gers, he resembled a bear torn from his hibernation nest. She patted his cheek, enjoying the rough texture, and he muttered darkly, "I like to sleep in the morning. Especially on my days off. That's difficult to do with you crashing around in here."

"I'm just rearranging a few things. You really need a new toothbrush, Sloan. What do you think?" She studied the razors and the separated shampoos.

"I think people sleep in the morning...especially on days off when it's raining," he gritted between his teeth. "You've been clattering around the place for a full hour."

"I've been putting away a few things. Then there was the dishes. The coffee and juice is ready—I'll just pop the rolls into the oven to warm. I've made a list of things I thought we could do to spend our time today...."

Sloan cursed, shortly and effectively. Melanie stared at him. "You are a beast in the morning, sweetheart," she said warningly. She decided to ignore his naked body. When he was in a better mood, she'd present him with a proper nightshirt. "Why don't you have breakfast...?"

He glared at her from beneath his brows and entered the bathroom to begin his shower. Steam filled the room. "I asked if you would like breakfast...?" Melanie prompted over the sound of the running water, resisting the urge to toss a cold glass of water into the shower.

Later, Sloan looked over his cards at her, sipped his coffee and asked, "You're really in a snit, aren't you, Mel?"

She laid a royal flush firmly between them and picked up her notebook and pencil. She began making lists for the reception, ignoring the way he slid the cards to the floor. Reluctantly she admitted that he was a good loser; when he won, it was with a dashing predatory flair. Sloan nudged her stocking-clad foot with his. "Eh, M.S.? In a little snit, are we?"

"You are a beast in the morning, Raventhrall," she repeated, adding a notation about mineral water and limes, and brushed away a crumpled fortune cookie wrapper from her jean-clad knee. Sharing the small couch with Sloan was like maneuvering around a very friendly bear in a small boat.

His toes nudged her hips insistently. "Okay, I take back that crack about neat phobias and demented women."

"You're a bed hog."

He brushed the curls at the back of her neck, wrapping a silky strand around his finger. "That's because you're so delectable and cuddly. You're a blanket hog."

She looked over her notebook primly. "One tends to accumulate blankets when they are constantly being tossed on one."

He laughed outright and gathered her onto his lap. "Give me that damned list, Inganforde, and tend my bruised heart."

"One cannot play the weekend away," she managed huskily before his lips brushed hers.

Eleven

Monday morning Sloan collected the napkin bits and the backs of envelopes bearing his notations, then slapped them into a file. Taped to the window, Danielle's new Christmas poster, portraying a skinny Santa Claus and doglike reindeer, fluttered as he turned to stare out at the light snow.

The startled, hungry sighs of Melanie's passion kept him constantly aroused. But Melanie hadn't totally committed to him. He sensed that she protected her essence from him, and the thought nagged and wounded. She'd been too quiet on the return trip, slipping into her apartment with an air of a nymph escaping to her bower to sulk. Itty and Delilah's reception next weekend would take an immense amount of her time, she explained when he asked if he could stay the night.

Inganforde was a tough nut to crack, setting up her defenses once she and Sloan returned to reality.

He began listing the means to make their arrangement more appealing; he began rolling the toothpaste tube from

the bottom. He wanted his bathroom cluttered with feminine bottles and scents.

Generally, Melanie Sue Inganforde remained a flower-
scented mystery. Sloan watched Danielle's dog-reindeer
thoughtfully.

Melanie had developed a predatory aura, as though she
were circling a quarry, listing its weaknesses before she
struck. Devereau had remarked that "Inganforde is showing signs of the old bird-dog trait. There's an account she
wants badly—something worth fighting for—and by Jove,
she's going to get it," he had crowed. "With two star players at Standards, we can boost our ratings...."

Leaning back in his desk chair, Sloan cracked open a fortune cookie and read, *One must wait for good fortune.*
"Damn," he muttered quietly, snapping open another
cookie. *Patience will bring your reward.* He munched on the
crumbs and traced Melanie as she walked to Georgette's
desk and leaned her hip against it. Dressed in a gray dress
suit and cream blouse, Melanie had added a spiffy, avant-
garde gold pin.

Sloan closed his eyes, remembering her pale, silky curves
clad in the black, revealing teddy.

Inganforde could be dangerous, unlike his sweet little
nymph. Inganforde was a contemporary woman on the career prowl. He wanted Melanie to be satisfied on both
fronts.

"A disaster waiting to happen," Sloan muttered as her
jacket shifted to reveal the voluptuous curves beneath. He
wanted to cuddle and pet and love M. S. Inganforde....

Sloan snapped a pencil in two and tossed it into his trash.

A cheery morning person, Melanie had discovered his
moody temper in dawn's light. If only he hadn't yelled when
the coffee began to perk and her spatula scraped the bottom of the skillet as she fried eggs.

Then there was the way he'd ripped her sweet little nightie
away, foraging for her delectable curves.

He'd shocked Melanie right down to her pink toenails when he suggested they share the tub. When she played poker in her nightgown, a frothy pink ruffled thing, he couldn't resist drawing her onto his lap.

Later, he'd made the mistake of chuckling as she straightened and organized their tangled, rumpled clothes. Horrified by the way he packed his luggage to return, she'd actually shuddered.

Sloan settled back in his chair to watch the Christmas shopping crowds mill through the streets. He'd made his moves; the next move was M. S. Inganforde's....

Melanie watched Sloan move through the Standards aisles. As a potential life-mate, he was uncomfortable and tense. Bodacious amazons lurked at every water fountain, brazenly peering at his pattable backside. She snapped a pencil and tossed it to the desk.

Loralee, a magnificent amazon, leaned against Sloan near the filing cabinets, and Melanie narrowed her eyes. Poor Sloan, an innocent among men, unaware of how certain females could take advantage of his sweet disposition.

Yet there was a savagery deep within him that Melanie longed to equal.

She wanted to meet him on every plane, professionally and in their relationship. Without doing the proper running, she would never feel truly comfortable with Sloan as a life-mate. She wanted to seduce him, compromise him and carry him away to his dream farm in Iowa, thus keeping his old-fashioned values unbesmirched.

Melanie tapped another pencil on her desk and slowly rubbed her stocking-clad toes against the smooth wood. A careful lover, Sloan gently urged her to passionate heights, then followed her as a gentleman would.

Loralee's white hand touched Sloan's broad chest, and Melanie straightened. Her temper rose as she crushed the growth-and-earnings charts which she had been skimming.

When the amazon's sexy blue eyes worshipped Sloan and he smiled in return, Melanie stood up and moved around her desk. She understood at that moment why Sloan had rescued her from Vinnie Perez and had been so angry at her potential seduction. She understood why Sloan had issued the "come and get me" challenge.

Life-mates and lovers needed to be captured and wooed and loved right out of their red-and-green stockings.

The father of her children needed her protection. Melanie smiled gently. Sloan would make a wonderful husband and father.

Melanie's frown returned as Loralee's bodacious bosom brushed Sloan's business jacket. Beneath his civilized veneer, Sloan was just an old-fashioned regular gentleman who needed protection from the female Vinnies of the world. She doodled across her Sloan list. She checked the word "savage," then darkened in the letters.

While Sloan wanted to cuddle and woo and protect, Melanie wanted something very different. She wanted...she wanted...to release every bit of her essence, exposing Sloan to the competitive woman deep within. Smiling slightly, Melanie recognized that Sloan had released a measure of her sensuality, had given her confidence to explore.

Poor Sloan. He treasured the idea of a sweet, pliable lover, and Melanie hadn't wanted to disillusion him. He enjoyed pursuing, wooing and seducing.

Would their love remain if she exposed him to her true emotions? Could Sloan withstand her if she released her inhibitions? Would he want her as desperately if she revealed her savage need of him?

Until Sloan had waylaid her, Melanie had allowed herself to drift into a routine of career and home projects. Now, with Sloan spread before her like a Sunday smorgasbord, she wanted to sample the heady invitation of her sensuality.

Though living with him would be an experience in survival—Melanie shuddered as she thought of the way he tossed silverware into a drawer in lieu of sorting it into its proper bins—Sloan was delicious, attentive and much more huggable than her pillow. With time, perhaps he could learn to play poker properly.

Melanie frowned, smoothing her new gold pin zigging across her lapel. It represented the new woman Sloan had unleashed....

Rick definitely could not have withstood the sensual onslaught she planned for Sloan. Melanie sighed wistfully, praying that Sloan would understand her need to balance their relationship. Her need to give as well as take.... *Could Sloan cope with her as an active, assertive lover?*

Tapping a message into her computer, she sent it to Sloan's office—*S. Jogging? Six a.m.? M.*

Within fifteen minutes, Sloan returned to his desk and sent his answer. *Yuck. Dinner? Dancing?*

Melanie shot back, *Lunch.*

At eleven-thirty, Melanie arrived at Sloan's office dressed in her winter coat and carrying a huge bouquet of lush red roses. "For you," she said, thrusting them at him.

Rising to his feet, Sloan pushed his hand through his hair and stared blankly at the flowers. "What's this?"

Melanie swallowed at his slightly defensive tone. "Flowers."

"For me? What am I supposed to do with them?" Sloan's raspy voice had a distinctive bristling tone. He ran his hand across his jaw with the air of a man caught amid a hoard of shopping women in a January white linen sale.

His vulnerability had never been more endearing, and it bolstered Melanie's confidence. "You gave me flowers," she whispered, standing up on tiptoe to kiss his chin. "I wanted to return the favor."

Sloan's dark eyes gleamed beneath his lashes, and Melanie sensed his intense pleasure. He softened immediately, squashing the bouquet between them as he gathered her into his arms. He kissed her hungrily as the fragrance of the crushed petals rose to surround them.

Lifting her until her lips were level with his, Sloan nibbled around the perimeters and breathed unevenly. "Gee, you know how to treat a guy, Inganforde," he whispered.

Throughout lunch, Sloan glanced at her repeatedly, and she noted the many times he ran his hand through his hair. Over the last dish of cheese and fruit, Sloan looked down at her hand as it toyed with the back of his. He turned his palm upward and watched her tapered nails delicately scrape his darker skin. "You could be starting something you can't finish," he said in a sensual drawl.

"Really?" Melanie allowed her hand to lower beneath the table and caressed his hardened thigh.

A flush ran beneath Sloan's dark skin. "Lay off, Mel."

Customers nearest their table turned when Melanie's low, sexy laughter rippled over the clatter of dishes and plates. She batted her lashes at Sloan. "Can't you take it?"

Saturday afternoon, Delilah and Itty's reception blended jitterbug music with country and western. A curious blend of people mingled near the giant frozen glove. An interesting little man wearing a long coat shoved up his sleeves to reveal an assortment of wristwatches to the guests.

Sloan cuddled Melanie in her teary relapses, though he sensed a dangerous living-on-the-edge mood in her at times. "Mother is protecting Itty's honor in a high stakes poker game tonight, and you're coming home with me," she whispered after patting his backside.

"It's nice to be needed," Sloan answered gallantly as Delilah passed them with a tray of Itty's special barbecued beef. She winked at her daughter whose wicked giggle rippled across the back of Sloan's neck, raising his hair. Her small hand delicately patted his bottom.

Later, Sloan smoothed Melanie's curls as they rested on his chest. He surveyed his uncertain emotions; he wanted

Melanie's love, wanted marriage, children and... He decided that Inganforde probably wasn't destined for that farm in Iowa.

"Sloan," she whispered against his nipple, her fingers prowling through the hair on his chest. "You are wonderful...understanding...gentle...." Her small foot prowled up his calf.

"But...?"

She nibbled on his taut flesh, licking the hard pebble until he groaned. Sloan stirred immediately, aroused; they had just dropped over a sensual cliff and were savoring the pink cloud on which they drifted. "I don't want to frighten you, darling...but I've been...worried if you..."

"Yes?" Sloan shifted, tilting Melanie's chin higher with his fingertip. He sensed a dramatic moment in their lifemate relationship.

Dark blue eyes, filled with his reflection, gazed up at him. Beneath the luxurious quilts, Melanie's small hand stroked his chest. "Sloan, you're sweet, but..."

"But?" Fear surged through him.

Melanie's soft, luscious body eased on top of him. She snuggled against him, nibbling on his earlobe. "I love you, darling, but..."

He inhaled sharply as her tongue flicked at his ear. With a pleased purr, Melanie took him into her. "But?" he asked unsteadily as she began to move against him in a fluid warmth.

"Ahh..." Melanie sighed, her body rippling sensuously, tensing in a quivery tight spasm. Her dark blue eyes prowled his chest hungrily, following the line of hair down his stomach and lower. She inhaled sharply and touched him gently with the tip of her finger. "I'm not...not...exactly what you think," she finished unevenly. "Oh, Sloan, I'm really a savage beast where you're concerned."

"Give, Inganforde. What's the problem?" Sloan ordered when he could speak. Passion pounded through him, hot and heavy, and he wanted to wait for Melanie. Her soft breasts nestled against him, their gentle pressure begging for the cup of his palms. The delicate contractions within her body were close to driving him over the edge. . . .

Sloan closed his eyes, anticipating the moment when her soft cries would be muffled by his shoulder, the exciting pressure of her nails gently pressed into his skin. A ballet of pale skin and delicate, quivering heat, Melanie was perfect—sweet and shy. An old-fashioned woman who starts a man's home fires burning. . . .

She moved valiantly onward, her hand skimming downward. Against his lips, she whispered, "You're so sweet, Sloan, so traditional. I'm afraid—" She shifted uncertainly, taking him deeper. "Oh, Sloan, I love you so, but if I show you how much, you'll be frightened—"

"I'll try to be brave, honey," he answered after closing his eyes and savoring the flow of her small, soft body against his.

Melanie fought to be sweet. Fought to be cuddly and traditional and gentle with Sloan. She suckled his bottom lip, nibbled at the corners of his firm mouth and stroked his trembling, deliciously lean and muscled body.

Could he withstand the rigors of her love? Should she unleash those savage impulses . . . ?

She lifted higher, savoring the crisp waves of hair sliding through her fingers, the sensually devastating gaze of Sloan's dark eyes. In an unscheduled burst of delight, Melanie cried out as his lips closed around the sensitive pebble of her breast.

"Heavens to Betsy," she whispered shakily as she moved into the fire, uncaring of Sloan's fragility. Later she must apologize. . . .

"Sweetheart, you are so sweet," Sloan whispered against her other breast, pressing her deeper against him. His mouth, hot and moist, suckled gently. The cords deep within her began vibrating hungrily.

Melanie strained to remember...something she had temporarily forgotten, but needed to tell him.

Filling her, uniting his body with hers, Sloan was her love, her other half into eternity.

Sweeping aside her last thoughts to preserve poor Sloan, Melanie tightened her body on his, braced her hands beside his on the violet-patterned pillowcase and soared.

Sloan survived her savagery magnificently. He didn't protest when she began a second seductive onslaught immediately after their shower. The buttons of his new brown-and-cream-striped nightshirt popped off easily beneath her anxious fingers....

Hours later, amid tangled ruffles and Sloan's hard, fit body, Melanie dozed lightly while he stroked her hair. "Melanie...sweetheart?" Sloan prodded gently.

His chest was slightly damp with his latest endeavor to withstand the rigors of her love, and Melanie nuzzled it pleasantly. "Mmm?"

"I've been wondering where you grew up. On a farm, according to your mother...."

She kissed his nipple, worrying it with her teeth. She remembered what she had wanted to tell Sloan. She finger-walked across a ticklish spot on his ribs, grinning as he squirmed. She smiled wickedly. "A farm in Iowa."

Four months later, Sloan and Melanie walked toward the Standards Elite building, each carrying their briefcases and dressed in business suits. He did not resemble the cuddly, rumpled lover of dawn who needed pampering until he adjusted to the day. Sloan was created for nightshirts, his hard thighs seductively exposed by the slit. A masculine confection, Sloan looked wonderful amid a four-poster bed scattered with rose petals.

Her list-making blended perfectly with Sloan's creative talents—after two cups of coffee and a loving kiss.

An intuitive star player, Sloan had helped to create their baby after a beautiful wedding thrown by Itty. Perhaps the baby was a result of her first attempt at a closet seduction just after the wedding. Sloan had been gorgeous, irresistible in a black tuxedo... His immaculate groom image had ached to be disheveled. A true gentleman, he hadn't protested as she'd taken his tie to draw him into the closet.

Sloan would react wonderfully to her news over a candlelight dinner. El Lobo was delighted, increasing his own effort to find a suitable life-mate. Danielle, after her stint as a flower girl, would finally have the baby cousin she wanted. Delilah would react in a soft grandmother's bloom, and Itty would...

Melanie hesitated at the "Itty would" level. Perhaps she should prepare a list of the "Itty woulds."

She closed her eyes, savoring the soft March breeze sweeping through her curls. Somewhere in Iowa, fathers were helping children make kites.... Her mother had deeded the farm to her as a wedding gift; Iowa would be a wonderful place to raise their children. With little effort, Sloan and she could open a financial service from their home.

She eyed Sloan shyly, imagining their child tucked safely in his arms, and found him looking down at her with that devilish gleam in his dark eyes. To deepen that expression, she licked her lips and found him staring hungrily at her. "I love you, Mel," he stated simply and with such intensity that she blushed.

Living with Sloan, an instant player, was delicious. With practice she could match his skill for picking the proper moments. Her list of proper moments was tucked in her briefcase; it needed fine-tuning to equal Sloan's creativity.

The bodacious amazons would have to play without him. A traditional, gallant lover, Sloan deserved cuddling and wooing. Because he responded wonderfully to her un-scheduled, seductive impulses, Melanie reached down to fondly pat his bottom....

* * * * *

If you've been looking for something a little bit different, a little bit spooky, let Silhouette Books take you on a journey to the dark side of love with

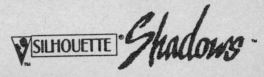

Every month, Silhouette will bring you two romantic, spine-tingling Shadows novels, written by some of your favorite authors, such as *New York Times* bestseller Heather Graham Pozzessere, Anne Stuart, Helen R. Myers and Rachel Lee—to name just a few.

In May, look for:
FLASHBACK by Terri Herrington
WAITING FOR THE WOLF MOON by Evelyn Vaughn

In June, look for:
BREAK THE NIGHT by Anne Stuart
IMMINENT THUNDER by Rachel Lee

Come into the world of Shadows and prepare to tremble with fear—and passion....

Take 4 bestselling love stories FREE

Plus get a FREE surprise gift!

INTIMATE MOMENTS®
10TH Anniversary

Celebrate our anniversary with a fabulous collection of firsts....

The first Intimate Moments titles written by three of your favorite authors:

NIGHT MOVES	**Heather Graham Pozzessere**
LADY OF THE NIGHT	**Emilie Richards**
A STRANGER'S SMILE	**Kathleen Korbel**

Silhouette Intimate Moments is proud to present a FREE hardbound collection of our authors' firsts—titles that you will treasure in the years to come, from some of the line's founding writers.

This collection will not be sold in retail stores and is available only through this exclusive offer. Look for details in Silhouette Intimate Moments titles available in retail stores in May, June and July.

SIMANNR

WHERE WERE YOU WHEN THE LIGHTS WENT OUT?

This summer, Silhouette turns up the heat when a midsummer blackout leaves the entire Eastern seaboard in the dark. Who could ask for a more romantic atmosphere? And who can deliver it better than:

**LINDA HOWARD
CAROLE BUCK
SUZANNE CAREY**

Look for it this June at your favorite retail outlet.

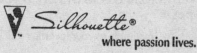

where passion lives.

SS93

Relive the romance...
Harlequin and Silhouette
are proud to present

by Request

A program of collections of three complete novels by the most requested authors with the most requested themes. Be sure to look for one volume each month with three complete novels by top name authors.

In June: **NINE MONTHS** Penny Jordan
                                   Stella Cameron
                                   Janice Kaiser

Three women pregnant and alone. But a lot can happen in nine months!

In July: **DADDY'S**   Kristin James
            HOME   Naomi Horton
                             Mary Lynn Baxter

Daddy's Home... and his presence is long overdue!

In August: **FORGOTTEN**   Barbara Kaye
            PAST   Pamela Browning
                            Nancy Martin

Do you dare to create a future if you've forgotten the past?

Available at your favorite retail outlet.

HARLEQUIN®   Silhouette